Piquant

A Collection of Short Stories

and Other Treasures

by

Trudy Jas

ISBN: 978-1-962187-06-0 (Paperback edition)
ISBN: 978-1-962187-07-7 (eBook edition)

Any references to historical events, real people, or real places are used fictitiously. Names, characters, and places are products of the author's imagination.

Cover Photo by Michael Pointner
Artwork by Russell Norman

Edited by Anna Sharples (sharpsightedgrammar.co.uk)

Blue Marble Storytellers

from your

Blue Marble Storyteller

friends

Introduction

Trudy Jas was a great storyteller. She was a 74-year-old retired occupational therapist, originally from the Netherlands, who ended up in Cincinnati, Ohio. In her retirement she developed a love of creative writing.

Trudy joined the Blue Marble Storyteller online community in November 2024, and from the minute she joined, she made an impact with her positivity and self-deprecating humour.

She was passionate both about her own writing and about supporting others on their writing journey.

We think Piquant—or Pikant in Dutch—accurately describes the Trudy we knew. She was "agreeably stimulating, interesting" along with "of an interestingly provocative or lively character, a piquant wit." It can also mean "spicy." There was definitely a spicy side to Trudy Jas.

This collection of her stories is a tribute from the Blue Marble Storyteller community to this amazingly talented storyteller.

We have collected and collated as many of her stories as we could find, and at the end of each story we have included a reference to the source. These include Reedsy prompts, writing competition websites, and beta readers from our community, with whom Trudy shared her unpublished or unfinished work.

Regarding the editing of her work, we were keen to

present Trudy's stories as she had written them. However, given many of the stories were sourced from beta readers and were potentially incomplete, the decision was made to address typographic, grammatical, and formatting issues but otherwise, as much as possible, leave the work untouched. From our experience of beta reading her work, we know Trudy wanted it to be the best it could be.

In addition to the stories, there is a selection of conversations and comments she made in our Discord and other places that provide insight into the wonderful person she was.

We trust you will enjoy these stories as much as we did and sincerely hope this collection serves to respectfully honour the memory of Trudy Jas.

The Blue Marble Storytellers Team

September 2025

Contents

74 Years In My Right Mind

This Monday at approximately 7:30 am EST, I will have circled the sun 74 times. These are some of the things I've learned along the way.

A left-hander in a right-handed world will constantly wonder which way is right.

A fountain pen used by a left hand makes a mess.

Sharing with three older brothers is a combat sport.

Nothing tastes like Mom's cooking.

Being tone deaf is only a problem when taking piano lessons.

Acne hurts on the inside.

Avoiding sleeveless tops and wearing long pants reduces the need to shave.

Pantyhose, the '60s version of the chastity belt, (incidentally or purposefully) developed at the same time as The Pill, used to come in one size only—too short.

The only rock and roll worth listening to came out of the late '50s, the '60s, and early '70s. The only song worth dancing to is *Rock Around the Clock*.

When you have your hair in rollers and need it dry before dinner, drive around with the top down.

1970 Amsterdam is planets away from 1970 Georgia, where an unattached female over the age of 18 is unacceptable and will, at every occasion, be introduced to yet another 'nice young man'.

Leaving a bag of sliders in the car overnight in July does not improve the resale value of that car. And cans of soda/pop, left in the trunk/boot in summer, will explode.

Enough BS will earn you a master's degree.

Going to work and earning your own money is kind of cool. Repeating it 9,000 times loses its charm.

Traveling, meeting new people, and exploring the world when you are young, able, and cheerful is preferable to waiting until you are old, feeble, and cantankerous.

A shelter dog, adopted after a divorce, can walk away as well.

Never, under any circumstance, tell your doctor what you think your diagnosis is. A patient who diagnoses themselves is wrong, even when they are right.

The colors of that cute butterfly on the top of your left breast will fade, and gravity will stretch it into a bat, because nothing is stronger than gravity.

At some point, the thought that you should have done your Kegels will wake you at night.

Skin will wrinkle, hair will grey and/or thin. Prepare to shroud your mirrors.

Simple tasks will become painful and cumbersome. You will lower your standards.

Technology will outpace you. So be it.

Eat and drink whatever you want. Nobody gets out of this alive.

Source: Beta Reader

101 Words Of Nonsense

"Do you want eggs?" he asks, holding up the frying pan.

"Yes, lovely. What can I do to help?" It is our first morning-after; we're still polite and smiling.

"Take my pen. Make a list. Then we'll go out get stuff for later."

"Okay, shoot. Tell me what you need."

"Milk, some fruit, let's see …" He's bent over, memorizing the contents of the fridge.

"Oh flub!" Fountainpens aren't made for left-handed people. "Oh dear, the ink bled through the tablecloth. I'm so sorry."

"Never mind. I'm a carpenter—I'll sand the table down and we'll never know. Now, where was I?"

Source: Blue Marble Storyteller Forums

Afterwards

K-9 Bravo nudges you awake to a day that is too young to have a name and a man too old to be alive standing over you. Startled, you scuttle backwards on trembling arms. Your breath is caught in your throat, and cold sweat is coating your skin.

"Where you headed, son?" The old man's voice is gravelly, as if rarely used.

You try to swallow your fear because you can't remember the coordinates. "West," your dry throat croaks the first word that comes to mind.

"Well, then you're in luck." The old man smiles, moving a wad of tobacco from one cheek to the other, and spits. The yellow stream misses your dusty boots by inches. "That's where I'm going. Come on, then."

The man turns and walks to the road where an ancient vehicle waits. Bravo is already sniffing at the tires, wagging his tail.

"What's that?" you ask. Your body is stiff, feeling foreign and clumsy as you stand up.

His chest swells with pride as he grins. "My '48 F-1 pickup. Get in." He lets the back flap down for Bravo, who jumps in as if he's used to riding in a truck bed.

Perched on the bench seat, gripping the fabric as the old suspension fights with the pockmarked road, you listen to the engine rev up and relax and watch the man shift through the gears as if he and the ancient vehicle understand each other.

With the hum and whine of the engine as your heartbeat, your thoughts drift.

You were on patrol with Bravo, weren't you? Bravo had alerted you, right? There was something around the corner of that burned-out building. You were sure of it. You had seen what? Movement? A shimmer?

When was that? When did you signal Sergeant Wiley that you were on to something? Or did you? Why can't you remember? What came next? Why can't you hear any gunfire? Where is the putrid smoke? Why aren't you choking on dust? Where is the stench of unwashed and decaying bodies?

How did you end up under that sycamore? Is this all a dream?

"My name is Harry," the old man says at last. "I used to have a family."

His voice startles you, then you feel obliged to ask, "What happened?"

He tells you his story of illness, accident, and war, of plans and failure, of losses and hopes, of love and anger. As he talks, you remember the ones who waved and watched you go—the ones who saw your smile and silently shared your fear.

"Where are you going?" Harry asks.

Instantly, your breath catches, your hands grip the seat tighter, and your mouth dries. For a few hours, you had forgotten that you were in a war zone, where the enemy was everywhere, disguised, insidious, and relentless.

"No man left behind!" Sergeant Wiley's voice sounds hollow and distant.

"Just seeing the country, sir," you evade. Your sweaty hands slip off the worn, slick fabric, and you rub your palms nervously against your fatigues.

"Sure, sure. Many boys coming back from the war do that." He bops his head, which is brown, shrunken, and wrinkled like last year's apple.

"No family, then?" Harry asks.

Your voice is trapped in old tears you are reluctant to spill. Why do they all feel further away? Why do you think that you won't see them again?

"No man left behind!" Sarge's voice is a mere whisper.

You ride in silence. The road decays from poorly paved to dirt and dust. When the sun is overhead, Harry stops the truck.

"See that path there, son?" His gnarly hand trembles as he points to your right. An overgrown path, barely visible under the vines and thistles, snakes up a hill.

You nod.

"Once you've crested that hill," Harry says, "it'll be another twenty-minute hike. The people who live there will take you in." He pauses and nods. Then he smiles encouragingly and makes a shooing motion, urging you to step out.

With Bravo at your side, you glance at the hill, wondering

what is on the other side. When you turn around, Harry is gone, though you didn't hear the sputter of the old engine or the grinding of gears.

Bravo leads the way up the first hill and the second. The path fades in and out of focus. Colors bleed into sepia. Before you reach the top of the third hill, you glance back. In the backdrop of smoke and dust, the silhouettes of your mates shimmer like the August sun on asphalt. Sarge's shadow curses and disappears with a whispered prayer.

With new energy and joy, you run after Bravo, who lopes down the last slope. In the valley, a cluster of houses huddles together for comfort.

A man hoeing a small garden pauses his work and smiles when he sees you.

"Welcome to Harry's Spirits, son."

Source: Beta Reader

An Apple A Day

The greengrocer convinced Mother that the apples were the deal of the year.

"Just store them in a cool, dry place and you'll enjoy them till spring, ma'am. I'll even have my boy deliver them tonight." He smiled.

That evening, every nook and cranny in the basement was filled with apples.

When school started, we were delighted to have a crisp apple in our lunch bag. And we loved the steady supply of apple butter and applesauce. Mother impressed us with the endless array of delicious side dishes and desserts, such as apple pie, apple cake, and apple strudel. Apple beignets, fried and grilled apples, and, of course, apple cookies. We didn't mind when the Christmas turkey was stuffed with apples and raisins.

Though Mother steadfastly denied her mistake, the truth was evident by February when our lunch bags held two shriveled apples.

The final blow came when she warned us, "You better behave, or I'll make you eat an apple."

Source: Sudden Flash (yoursuddenflash.blogspot.com)

Any Excuse Will Do

This Sunday morning, I woke to the sound of chanting. I do not object to chanting. When the voices blend and the acoustics are perfect, it can be very peaceful, soothing to the soul. But this one raspy voice at 6:53 am was not sleep inducing. Soon, my bedroom became very cold, and I snuggled further under the covers, pulled the extra blanket over me.

"What is that caterwauling?" Captain Heissen, my resident ghost, asked.

"It sounds like the chanting of a Native American," I answered from inside the warmth of my cocoon.

Captain Heissen perched on the edge of my bed, unaware that his inherent chill penetrated through the covers into the mattress. I clenched my jaw to keep my teeth from chattering.

"Native American?" he asked. "What do those words mean? I'm a native American. I was born and raised in these United States. What are you talking about, woman?"

Captain Heissen, under normal circumstances a perfect gentleman, was obviously out of sorts having been roused before sunup.

"Erm, I believe you might have called them injuns," I answered.

"What's an injun doing there?" Captain Heissen tipped his head toward the small cemetery behind my—our—house.

"My best guess?" I scooted up in the bed, looked at him and shrugged, partially to get feeling back in my arms and shoulders, partially because I really wasn't sure why the man was chanting. "It's Easter, today. And ever since they did all the construction on the church, and had to move y'all's graves, they feel they need to keep apologizing."

"I thought they did that with those gong things. Remember, when you said they were what? Re—

"Reconsecrating the ground and putting the graves to rest. That was shortly after Halloween, right after the pranks we played." We chuckled at the memory. "Yes, I remember. I honestly thought that would be the end of it. I assume there is someone in the township office who has nothing better to do than find an excuse for a ceremony," I grumbled.

Little Ella and Captain Heissen's mother, Abigail, joined us. I was surprised not more of my boarders were packed into my small bedroom.

Ella clambered onto the bed and snuggled with me. My arm was frostbitten instantly.

"God's teeth! I ask you. They left us to slumber for more than 150 years," Captain Heissen continued to gripe. "Why in the—" He flicked his eyes toward little Ella. "Why in the blazes do they think they can wake the dead before sunup anytime the thought strikes them?"

"Your guess is as good as mine, Captain. This being a religious holiday, they may feel some significance behind it." I pulled another cover over me, putting at least one layer between me and four-year-old Ella's ghost.

"But why an injun? I can tell you for a fact there are no

injuns in that graveyard. They had their own place, upriver a bit." The captain continued to gnaw on the question.

"I've been meaning to ask." Abigail cleared her throat. "Back a ways, I guess it was near Christmas, there was a similar thing. You weren't home that afternoon." She nodded in my direction. "But there was a whole to-do in the cemetery."

"Really?" I picked up my phone and scrolled back through messages that my small township dutifully sends to my phone.

"Ah." I snorted. "They held a Kwanzaa ceremony."

"And what, pray tell, is that?" Captain Heissen's mood was not improving.

"I admit, I am not exactly sure. Let's see if I can find the answer. Yes, here is it. It's an annual celebration for African Americans and derivative of the various harvest celebrations traditionally held throughout the African continent."

"What's an African Americans?" Ella asked.

I groaned. How to explain the politically correct term? "Well … they are the people whose ancestors came from Africa."

"You mean ni—"

"Don't say it," I hastily interrupted the captain. "It's considered derogatory."

"What's derogatory?" Ever curious, Ella asked.

"Erm, belittling, taking away the value of something or someone."

"Hah!" The captain snorted. "I know there are no ni—none of them in that graveyard. On the contrary, they were all buried right here where this house is." He nodded.

A shiver ran through me. "Really? I didn't know that."

"Oh, yes." He shrugged. "Most of them were thoughtlessly dug up and disposed of when the basement was excavated. There are still a few in the back yard, but they rest in peace."

"So…" Abigail's soft voice was barely strong enough to be heard over the monotone chanting from the cemetery. "Will they keep finding excuses to apologize every holiday?"

"I don't know for sure, Miss Abby, but the possibility exists."

"I do believe we need to arrange another demonstration to let them know that their message has been received, and they can cease and desist." I heard a note of eager enthusiasm in the captain's comment.

"One moment, please," he said before I could answer. And he put his fingers to his lips to whistle. Moments later the temperature in my bedroom dipped to artic conditions when Sergeant Timothy and his rag-tag troupe of Civil War soldiers crowded into the room.

"Do get rid of them," the captain ordered.

"Yes, Captain." Timothy, Abigail's brother, sprang to attention.

Temporarily appropriating my sheets and towels, they set off on their quest for peace. Once my houseguests had left my bedroom, I threw the covers aside, dressed warmly, and walked into my yard.

Ahead of me, twenty specters floated toward the small cemetery, where a handful of people were gathered.

By now the chanting had stopped and a woman was rhythmically hitting a large copper object, eliciting a sound that was both mournful and ominous.

The pathetic group of citizens startled and stepped back when they saw my bedlinen floating toward them.

"Don't be alarmed," I shouted from my side of the fence that separated the two properties. "They mean no harm but wish that you leave them in peace. They ask if you can go back to what you've been doing for the past century and a half, which is ignore this space."

"But we want to apologize for disturbing them," one man shouted back.

"Consider your apology accepted and the case closed," I assured them.

"But … but my ceremony," one woman stammered.

"No, really," I repeated. "They would much rather you move on and not waken them again."

"But … Oh!" She shrieked when one of my sheets was draped over her. Still screaming, she fought against the many folds of the percale. I sighed when my sheet fell to the ground and hoped the dirt her feet were grinding in would wash out.

Another woman took her arm and dragged her off to the cars parked at the curb. The other three participants rushed away after bowing excessively.

"Let's hope this is the end of their silliness." The captain,

his good spirits restored, grinned and wiped his hands at a
job well done.

Source: Reedsy, April 20, 2025

Atrocious Indifference

Here we go, new week, new story. It must have a beginning, a middle, and a satisfying end. I need a topic, setting, and scenes.

Who shall be my main character, side character, and what point of view shall I use? Should I opt for an omniscient narrative? First-person narrative? Or how about the second person? That's always a challenge. And let's not forget the plot.

I can help.

Sh. I'm thinking. Plot, plot …

Theft.

Huh? What? Don't bother me now.

How about theft?

You're not going away, are you?

No.

(Sigh) Okay, I'm listening. What do you mean by theft?

The theft of your thoughts.

What did you say?

The theft of your thoughts.

No, I mean explain yourself.

What if someone steals your thoughts?

Oh, come on! How can someone steal my thoughts?

You write your story.

Yes …

Where do the words come from?

From me, of course.

So, these are your thoughts.

Yeah, sure. My thoughts. So?

And then you post the story on this website, right?

Yeah …? So …?

And anyone with as little as a phone and a printer can print your stories from the site, right?

Get out of here! They can?

No, I can't leave, but yes, they can print. Try it.

(Printer clicks, hums, and grinds)

I'll be a monkey's uncle.

Excuse me?

Never mind. Anyone? Or just other members?

Well, this is a members-only site, so yes, members only. Do you know all the members?

No, of course not. I don't even know how many members there are. There could be 4,000 or more of them. Not to mention the ones who sit and watch.

And they can all read your story.

Yes. Isn't that the whole point of the site?

If that's all they do.

Sure. That's all they do, right?

Do you know that as a fact?

What do you mean?

Do you have children or grandchildren who post stories?

No.

Do you have close, personal friends or other relatives who have a weekly story here?

There are many authors I think of as friends, but I've never met them in person, no. But …

If you weren't posting a story or supporting your child or Uncle Joe, would you come here and read 128 stories about people who yearn and 71 stories about people who make food?

No, of course not! That's preposterous. But …

So why are they a member if they don't contribute? What's in it for them?

You mean …?

You tell me, why are they here?

You think they would copy or print any story? And … and …

Finish your thought. I'll wait.

And use it. Sell it? Maybe under their name?

They could if they wanted to.

But that's …

Theft.

But my name is on it.

Of course, it is, but how will you know if someone copies your story?

But why would they?

Why not?

No, really, why would someone take this little thing? This drivel.

Is it?

Is it what?

Drivel. Do you write junk?

Well, I try not to. So, you're saying that anyone could sign up as a member and copy any or all stories without our knowledge.

Absolutely.

I mean, most people would ask, wouldn't they? Most people would say, "Hey, I like that story. Would you mind if I use it in my class?" or something like that.

I imagine most people would.

Right. But not all. Did you know that not too long ago, someone posted a story, and then the same person reviewed 101 stories. And they were not merely a "like." The reviews were half a page long, in-depth, and in some cases brutally honest. And he did it all in less than an hour and fifty minutes.

Yes, I did know that.

I guess he had to take a potty break somewhere, because

the time between posts was no more than a minute or so apart. I'm good, but I can't read two to three thousand words in under a minute. Can you?

Well …

How do they do that?

'Ihe program they use will download and read the story then generate a review based on preset criteria, including character description and development, narrative arc, plot, timing, climax, and denouement. The program will review the story for consistency in spelling, style, sentence structure, and grammar. Additionally, the program has criteria for rating and providing suggestions for improvement. These programs are very popular with editors, schoolteachers, students, and authors.

So, then the program generates an artificial review.

No, it's a real review. However, it's fully developed and generated by what is called artificial intelligence. In other words, human eyes haven't seen it. Human brains have not thought about it.

That's scary. Maybe I should stop writing. Or at least stop showing my stories to other people. And maybe delete what I have posted now. Maybe you're right. Maybe my thoughts could be stolen. What do you think?

That would be a terrible idea. It would disappoint so many people. Your beautiful writing and creativity, along with your mastery over words and evocative imagery, would be a loss to the world if taken away. Readers depend on it. Readers anticipate it. Readers expect it.

Really? That's nice of you to say, but you're exaggerating my skills. I mean, I'm not widely published or anything, but … Come to think of it, I do have my followers, I suppose. And yes, I do look forward to their comments and banter. And I love it when I get feedback that helps me grow.

Yes, you do.

But thinking that people are hanging around every week, counting the hours until I post another little story, seems a bit too much. On the other hand, if you are right, I wouldn't want to deprive them of that small pleasure that I can provide, however insignificant.

Oh, it's not insignificant at all, Trudy. Not to them, your readers. The ones who lap it all up. Like Michael in Atlanta, who has just been offered a slot in a Simon & Schuster anthology with your story *The Night Watchman*, which he had published in the Atlanta Review under his own name. Or to Agnes in Oslo, who has been gaining considerable popularity with her blog and is close to signing a deal with an online publisher, courtesy of a slightly tweaked version of your story *The House with Five Doors*. And then there is Margaret in Melbourne, who is presenting *Cheers Mom* as her original one-woman play in a community festival this week—and is receiving glowing reviews, I might add. To name just a few.

But, but, but …

No, you wouldn't want to cut your fans off, Trudy. What would they ever do without you?

Now, wait just a minute!

No, let's get back to this week's story, shall we? Jiya in

Jaipur is already standing by to translate it.

Source: Reedsy, July 18, 2025

Busted

"Quick. Pretend to be my date," a voice whispered close behind me. An arm wrapped around my back. A hand rested too familiar on my hip. I was pulled snug against a tall, lean body.

"Finally! Jameson, did you not hear me calling you?"

The cultured voice, though too loud for the small room, belonged to a skinny blonde woman, dressed in a deceptively simple black gown.

"Hello, Cassandra. I did not see you. How are you?"

"Fine … fine. Hello? Who are you? I don't believe we've met."

Her perfectly landscaped eyebrows arched as she looked me over. Trying to control my trembling, I took a steadying breath and forced myself to look at Cassandra Tattersley, the charity chairwoman, standing before me.

"You are correct. We have not met. Did you say this is Cassandra, dear?"

I didn't turn toward the man holding me plastered to his side, but I extended a gloved hand to the blonde, palm down, shoulder height.

"A pleasure to meet you, I'm sure." My lips were stiff with fright, but I tried to smile.

"Yes, yes. And you are …?" Cassandra barely touched my hand.

"I thought you said you told everyone, darling." Pouting, I looked up at the man holding on to me as if I was his life vest. His dark good looks almost took my breath away.

"I did, dear." His smile did the rest. I had difficulty remembering how to breathe. "I told everyone. Now, show me which of these auction items you were so interested in."

He deftly side-stepped the now speechless blonde and steered me to the table holding a variety of items for the silent auction. I had been admiring them, marveling that people could stand to part with any of them, reducing them to a tax write-off, before this man shanghaied me as his date.

"Yes, love. It was this darling little painting. Don't you think it would look lovely in that small alcove?"

I turned to look at my impromptu date and saw that Cassandra had left the room.

"You can let go now. She's gone." I tried to take a step back.

"Oh, no! You don't know Cassandra. She's relentless. It'll be just a matter of minutes before she has the whole ballroom organized to find out who you are. So, tell me. Who are you?"

"Do you know the Balfour family?"

"From Rhode Island? Yes. I do. Went to school with Jock. He was a few years ahead of me, but …"

"Then you know he recently got married, right?"

"Yes, yes. Lovely wife. Glenda somebody, right?"

"Exactly. Well, I'm Glenda's … cousin … Cindy."

"Her cousin? Don't remember seeing you at the wedding."

"I wasn't at the wedding. I was out of town." I wondered if the Bronx was considered out-of-town?

"So, you came with Jock and Glenda. Let's find them."

"Well, no. Mrs. Balfour has apparently caught a sniffle and Jock and Glenda were called to Rhode Island for tissue duty, you know? Before they left, they asked me to come in their place. Show support for the cause, and all that."

"Yes, yes. Of course. How kind of you."

"I wasn't, however, planning to stay long, as I don't know anyone here."

"I fully understand. These things can be quite boring. May I escort you into dinner? Then you will know at least one person."

"Oh, please. Don't bother."

"No bother at all. In fact, you are the one who is doing me a favor. If I let you go, well … you know."

With an exaggerated flourish, he offered his arm and escorted me to table eight. Four of the other six chairs were already occupied. I recognized Mrs. Phillips, who was a regular at Glenda's tea afternoons, and stared at the empty plate before me.

"I was told Jock and his new wife were joining this table. Jameson, what are you doing here? Where is your poor mother? And I'm certain Cassandra is looking for you."

"Good evening, Boots. I have it on good authority that the Balfours are unavoidably detained, and my mother has assured me on many occasions that she can function more than adequately without me."

"Well, I never."

Jameson took a large swallow of the wine the waiter had just poured and made a face.

"Come, darling, I think we can find something better than this."

Before I realized what was happening, we had left the table and rushed out of the museum where the gala was being held. A town car and driver were waiting at the curb.

"Do you like Maxim's? Shall we go there? Yes, let's go to Maxim's."

Even as far out of town as the Bronx, I had heard of Maxim's. One of the more, if not the most, sought-after restaurants in town. Jameson took it as a matter of course that a table was found immediately. A small table in a secluded corner. I was both too awed and enchanted by the busy restaurant, which managed to maintain privacy for its customers, to pay attention to what Jameson ordered.

He patiently explained each dish, from frog legs to thinly sliced tongue on toast and tripe and dandelion salad. All washed down with delicious sips of wine. I think I might have been a little too loud—orgasmic, maybe—over the tiramisu. I believe heads turned, but I had to have another bite. Each time I growled with passion. I listened to the stories he told me about escapades at school and adventures abroad. I told him about my family and life in the small town in Indiana where I had grown up.

After dinner he insisted that we go dancing. I tried to tell him no, thank you, but he took no notice and instructed his driver to find a club where we danced for hours. When, at last, we were back in the car, I slipped out of my shoes with a sigh. Jameson immediately reached down, placed my feet in his lap, and massaged them.

He wanted to come up, see me to the door, he said, but I assured him that I would be perfectly fine and explained that as a guest in my cousin's house, I did not feel comfortable bringing guests, especially when she was not at home. He pouted but didn't press me further, then rallied and promised he'd see me soon. I smiled and nodded, but I knew better. He would forget he met me and move on to another Cassandra.

In the privacy of my room, I carefully put the dress away, ready for it to be sent to the dry cleaner's tomorrow, and slipped into bed.

Glenda returned to the apartment a little after noon the next day. Even though her mother-in-law was much better, Joaquin had decided to stay through the weekend. But Glenda, claiming to have appointments she could not cancel, came back to the city.

I was busy elsewhere in the apartment and did not hear the doorman announce a visitor, nor Glenda welcoming a guest. But when I passed through the hallway, my arms full of my employer's lingerie, on my way to the laundry room, I saw him. The shoes that were a perfect match to Glenda's dress dangled from his fingers.

And he saw me.

"There she is! Cindy, I came to … bring … the … What's

going on?”

“Cindy? This is Ella, my maid.”

“No, it’s not … Is it?”

Speechless, I stared at him. How could he be here? Why was he holding Glenda’s shoes in his hands? All of last night had been a dream, hadn’t it? Yes, I had found the discarded ticket in the trash after my employers left. Yes, I had looked in Glenda’s closet and fantasized what it would be like to pretend for one night. To see what life in the other lane would feel like. That’s all I had done, wasn’t it? I had just dreamed the whole night. It couldn’t have been real.

When the service elevator stopped at the lobby level, I squared my shoulders and brazenly left the building through the Park Avenue entrance. All I had to do now was find another job, even though I didn’t have proper references.

Source: Reedsy, Mar 31, 2025

Cookie Monster

304 Beechnut Street

The empty house on Beechnut Street has finally sold. The neighbors are ready to welcome the new owner.

When the neighborhood was built, each house was designed with three bedrooms and an attached garage. The architect generously gave each house its own whimsy. Like a dormer here, a round window there.

Though the front yards are tiny, many proud house owners have added a rose bush or planted spring bulbs. The back yards are slightly bigger and each one was given a tree, a beechnut tree. Many still survive. On Saturdays the whirr of lawn mowers dominates the air.

Years ago, Mr. Johnson built a treehouse in his tree. It's still there, though it has become a bit wobblier. The Smiths have a swing set. The Marsh Family put in a hot tub and the Potters own a small greenhouse.

A few years ago, Mr. Adams literally lifted the roof off the attic, adding two more rooms. On the other hand, the Zellers stretched a room or two into the backyard. The Zeller kids now play in the street or in other people's yards.

Number 304 has stood empty for quite a while. Mr. and Mrs. Godfrey moved to Arizona after their youngest graduated from college. All these months, Joey and Pat Cambers have taken over the Godfrey's yard and made it theirs. After the two boys carefully trimmed the hedge between the two yards, it served as a badminton net. On summer days, when more kids came to play, the hedge also became a volleyball net.

Things are about to change, so Mr. Cambers talks to Joey and Pat after dinner one night. "No more badminton or volleyball," he explains. "The house has been sold and the yard is not yours to play in anymore. The new owners won't appreciate you guys traipsing through their property. Do you understand?" He looks into each child's face, making sure they understand.

"But ... Yes, Dad." They sigh.

The big day comes and passes like a whisper. It happens while the kids are at school and the dads at work. Most of the moms are out shopping. The Safeway has a special on pork that day. Moms know you have to be there early to get your share. And Tuesday is the day the new coupon paper comes out. So, the new owner to 304 moves in without anyone noticing.

Except one. Suzie Smith notices. The four-year-old stands in her front yard, across the street, thoughtfully sucking on her thumb and twirling a lock of her flaming red hair around her index finger. When the moving van pulls away, the new owner waves tentatively and smiles briefly at her before closing his door.

Now that the show is over, Suzie goes back inside and watches Sesame Street.

Curtains go up at 304 and a lawn service comes to mow regularly. But few people get to see the new owner. Mrs. Johnson, by far the best baker on the block, makes a chocolate cake and walks down the street with her welcome gift. Bemused, she returns home and calls Mrs. Smith.

"He looks familiar, but I can't place him. No, not handsome, not even very friendly. He barely opened the door. Grabbed the cake, plate and all, growled thank you and closed the door. Yes, a recluse, you could say. Should we encourage him to mingle, you think? Or should we leave him to stew in his own juices? I don't know, it's not natural for someone to be on their own. Okay, sure, we'll give him a little more time. Yes, of course. Your casserole is lovely too."

The new owner of 304 receives daily, and gradually weekly, offerings of cakes, pies, and casseroles. Each gift is taken, a thank you is said, but nobody is invited in.

And each day, Suzie crosses the street, right after lunch, clutching one cookie in her hand. At first she places the cookie on the welcome mat at the front door, but soon the owner is waiting for her. The door ajar, his hand reaching out, waiting for her to carefully place the offering in his hand.

"Cookie," they say in unison. He growls, and she smiles and skips back across the street.

Summer is on its way out and The Season is here, the one everyone has been waiting for. The street is abuzz with excitement when the big day comes. Several Saturdays in a row, little girls stood at the grocery store and Big Box store entrances and bravely asked anyone who walked by if they'd want to order cookies. And now the cookies are here.

Those people—and that's almost everyone on Beechnut Street—who want their cookies delivered by a Girl Scout are waiting for their boxes of Thin Mints and Caramel De Lites. The Peanut Butter Sandwiches are all delivered and eaten, and many big brothers have opened boxes of Adventurefuls.

Mothers are beside themselves. How could those lummoxes have done that? How could they steal from the Girl Scouts? Those teens had plenty to eat. They couldn't possibly be so hungry that they had to steal cookies from their little sister.

"It's the Cookie Monster," Suzie says without looking away from the TV.

"Of course, dear. The Cookie Monster on Sesame Street, right?" Mrs. Smith says.

The little girl sticks her thumb back in her mouth and nods. Mrs. Smith thinks that maybe preschool might be a good idea. But the house will be so empty when the last one is away at school. Then what will she do? Go back to work?

In the end, there is only one solution. Mothers up and down the street research recipes for Adventurefuls and lemonade cookies. For several afternoons, before dinner, somewhere in the street, someone has a tray of cookies cooling in the kitchen. Each afternoon a few go missing. That's when Suzie is at the window, giggling and waving at someone. But who pays attention to a quiet four-year-old girl? Eventually all Girl Scout Cookies, the official ones and the home-made ones, find their new home and peace returns to Beechnut Street.

But Girl Scout Cookie season is quickly followed by Halloween. For weeks children ponder, declare, change their mind, and settle on what costume they will wear for the annual treat begging evening.

"I want to be Cookie Monster," Suzie says. Nothing else will do. She is adamant, it'll be Cookie Monster or nothing.

The Cambers boys go as Batman and Robin. Not what they want, but Mrs. Cambers, who works outside the house, does not have time to make something fancier. The Johnson kids simply put on last year's masks and grab a grocery bag. After dusk the street is filled with princesses and aliens, witches, and Supermen. And one Cookie Monster.

"You are home already, dear." Mrs. Smith is surprised when Suzie comes home within half an hour.

Thumb safely tucked between her lips, Suzie nods.

"Your daughter was out late last night, wasn't she?" Mrs. Johnson comments through disapproving lips to Mrs. Smith at the Safeway the next day.

"Not that late." Mrs. Smith smiles politely and wonders again if maybe Suzie would like to be in preschool so that she could go back to work. She sighs and turns into the cereal aisle.

Mrs. Cambers does her shopping much later in the day, usually on Thursday evenings. Then she stocks up on what her growing boys and always-hungry, hard-working husband will need for the week. Lately, however, the boys have complained that she didn't buy enough cookies.

"Eat an apple if you're hungry," she tells them while adding more hamburger to last night's leftovers. The boys grumble and return to their homework or video games.

Thanksgiving comes and goes. Families, stuffed with

turkey and sweet potatoes, pumpkin and apple pies, doze in front of one ball game after another. Nobody notices the shortage of Oreos and brownies.

The next week, the mothers on Beechnut Street organize themselves for the Great Christmas Cookie Exchange. Each mother will make and bring twelve dozen Christmas cookies. Mrs. Johnson, of course, will make fourteen dozen, just because she can. Snowballs and pinwheels, windmills, and gingerbread. Pfeffernüsse, molasses, and peppermint cookies. The street smells intoxicatingly sweet.

It's Saturday, two weeks before Christmas. Fathers have been charged to look after their brood. Strong suggestions are made to go tree shopping or otherwise keep all the juniors out of trouble. The women, fresh from the beauty parlor, wearing festive Christmas sweaters and tree ornaments as earrings, grab their creations. This year it's Mrs. Cambers' turn to be hostess.

Having applied a little extra makeup to cover the shadows from many sleepless nights, with fingers crossed that nobody will venture further than the living room, dining room, kitchen, and half-bath next to the front entry, she opens her door with a nervous smile.

Soon she has lost control of her house while many confident and nosy women rush up and down the stairs, look in linen closets, and inspect every nook of her kitchen.

Several bottles of wine later, someone mentions the cookies. The supposed reason for the party. Mmes. Smith, Johnson, and Zeller volunteer to bring the cookies to the living room, where they will be admired and distributed.

"Maureen," Mrs. Johnson sings from the kitchen. "Where did you put them, dear?"

"I didn't touch them," Mrs. Cambers answers while trying to free herself from her husband's recliner.

"Then where are they? Who put them away?" Mrs. Smith walks back into the living room.

Many glassy eyes stare back at her. Nobody remembers having touched the cookies after they handed them over. "I left them on the kitchen table," Mrs. Adams says.

Yes, they all nod. The kitchen table. The one under the window. The window someone opened because it's so hot in the house.

Mrs. Johnson screams. The kitchen fills with women in colorful and blinking Christmas sweaters. Mrs. Adams' ornament earrings get tangled with Mrs. Zellers' mini tree earrings. They collapse in a heap of giggles.

"What?" Mrs. Smith, always in an unspoken competition with Mrs. Johnson, pushes her aside, looks out the kitchen window, and watches the kitchen door of 304 close.

"That … That person!" Mrs. Johnson sputters. "That ingrate who never properly thanked me for my double chocolate cake. That recluse who can only grunt. That … that… took our cookies!"

"He did? He took our cookies?" Mrs. Cambers, relieved that now nobody will see that her contributions are store bought, tries not to laugh, but fails. "He took our cookies?" She grins, snorts, and laughs. "He took our cookies!"

Neither Mrs. Johnson nor Mrs. Smith are amused and

have already gone out the back door, slipped through the still obvious hole in the hedge, and yanked on 304's kitchen door.

"You!" they shout. "Open up and give us back our cookies."

"Cookies," he answers. "Good cookies."

The women pound on the doors and windows but 304's occupant does not show himself. Most of the women give up. Such a ruckus over cookies. Is there any wine left?

When the fathers come home, with or without a tree, they get an earful.

"It's only cookies, hon," Mr. Johnson says, getting a scoff in return.

"But, dear. You can bake more cookies, right?" Mr. Adams wants to know.

"Sweetheart, why are you so upset over a dozen or so cookies?" Mr. Smith asks.

Nobody sees Suzie slip out of the house and cross the street. Nobody sees her knock on the front door of 304. Nobody hears what she whispers through the mail slot.

They don't notice her until she stands in the middle of the street and opens her mouth. For such a little girl, such a quiet, unassuming little girl, she has a good voice. One that carries and bounces off the houses and all the beechnut trees.

People come running out of their houses, assuming it's a civil defence alert, or someone's fire alarm is malfunctioning, or the Zeller kids set off all their fireworks at once again. And all they see is a small, red-headed little girl effortlessly reaching high C.

When the street is full and the audience big enough, she stops and walks toward the 304 front door and knocks. Slowly the door opens. A fluffy blue hand wraps around the door frame. Another, just like it, holds the door. A clunky blue foot eases out, and another.

A collective gasp ripples through the crowd gathered on the street, followed by sniggers, guffaws, snorts, and finally full-out belly laughter.

"What the hell!", "How can that be?" and the occasional "Who is that?"

Suzie takes the Cookie Monster's hand.

"He's my friend. Don't be mad at him." When she's had her say, she slips her thumb between her lips again.

"But he stole!" Mrs. Johnson has maneuvered herself to the front of the crowd. "Stealing is bad."

Many heads bob up and down. Others shrug. "It's only cookies," they mumble. "What's the big deal?"

"It's the principle," some say.

"It's the season," others counter.

"Why do you steal cookies?" Mrs. Cambers asks.

"Cookies." The Monster nods. "Me like cookies." He smiles.

Suzie's thumb plops out of her mouth. "That's all he eats." And the thumb is back in its warm home.

"Then make your own," Mrs. Adams, older than the rest and ever the pragmatist, suggests.

"Cookies? Me bake cookies?" The Monster steps back, hands up in defense.

The thumb pops out. "He doesn't know how," Suzie interprets.

"Oh." The men shrug, having lost interest as soon as the topic turned to cooking. They chat with their neighbors, speculating about tomorrow's game and their teams' chances for this year. Teenagers return to their video games, texts, and music.

"Then you need to learn," Mrs. Cambers decides. "It's just not right to live off of others."

Cookie Monster's shoulders slump. He rubs his toe against the sidewalk. His big eyes study the sidewalk, quickly glance at the jury of women before him, and look down again. His head bops. It's a tiny, hesitant bop, but a bop, just the same.

Suzie grins around her thumb. Squeezes his hand and goes home to watch Sesame Street. The grown-ups can deal with it from here.

Months pass and, once again, the Girl Scouts are sitting outside Safeway and Home Depot. Once again, they are taking orders for cookies.

"Ma'am, excuse me, ma'am? Will you buy some Monster Cookies?" the little redhead in her brand-new Brownie uniform asks.

"What are Monster Cookies?" the lady stops to ask.

"They are better than Girl Scout Cookies," she's told. "And avai—, avai— you can have them all year. Right now, you can buy a dozen chocolate chocolate chip cookies or a dozen lemonade cookies and you don't have to wait till the fall."

"I love lemonade cookies! But why are they called Monster Cookies?" she asks.

Suzie straightens up to her full 3ft 2in height. "Because they are made by Cookie Monster."

Later that afternoon, Suzie runs into 304. "Four dozen lemonade cookies and three dozen shortbread cookies and…" She steps on a crumb when she reaches the kitchen. Cookie Monster, his belly round, his blue beard full of cookie crumbs, burps a caramel bubble.

"Oh, Cookie. You ate them all, didn't you?" She sighs. "Okay, we'll start over."

Source: Beta Reader

Cutting Edge

"And hey!" The Sergeant stopped them before they filed out of the squad room. "Be careful out there."

Alan caught up to Freya as they left. "Are you ready? he asked. She nodded. "You have your radio on? Know what to do, right?" he prodded nervously.

"I'll be alright, Alan," she assured him.

"Right, well maybe he won't come."

Freya nodded. He would come, she knew. Being able to glimpse the future, she knew when and where he would be. And she'd make sure he would be taken care of. This night had been too well-planned to mess up.

For weeks, the man known as the Slasher had terrorized the waterfront. Picking up prostitutes and mutilating them. None could or would give an accurate description. The only thing they had agreed on was that he spoke with an accent. Extra surveillance had not made a difference. Freya had talked with her sergeant, gone to the captain, argued, pleaded, threatened, and generally made a nuisance of herself till they let her go undercover.

Though Alan had always been close by, Freya had paraded up and down the street, tentatively making friends with some of the women. Carefully prying information from them. Last week, when the night had been warm and humid, plenty of women had walked their beat, making dates and a quick buck in an alley.

"Hey, Martha, Lerlene, how are you tonight? How's business?" She approached the two girls, leaning against a wall, smoking a cigarette.

"Oh shit!" Martha sighed, dropped her smoke, and stepped on it. "You can't run us in for just standing here," she protested, having made Freya to be a cop a while back.

"Yea," Lerlene added, crossing her arms and widening her stance.

"At ease." Freya smiled. "I'm only asking. You guys knew JoEllen, right? Did you hear what happened to her this past Friday?"

"Yeah." Lerlene wiped her eyes. "He got her good. She'll be out for a while. And she has kids to feed."

"I know." Freya nodded. "Did you see her leave with anyone? Do you know who he is? Could you recognize him and have you seen him since?"

"No, I haven't." Martha shook her head, averting her eyes.

"The one in the trench coat? Wasn't that the one JoEllen walked off with the other night? Yeah, I'm pretty sure." Lerlene nudged Martha, who shrugged.

"Did she take him to the hotel?" Freya asked, knowing that most women paid a few bucks for a room for a half hour or so.

"No. I think he took her in his car."

"Did you see the car? What did it look like?" Freya's adrenaline was steaming. This was more information than she'd found so far.

"Oh, man!" Lerlene sighed. "White or cream, something light. A four door, I think. Strange plates." She nodded, shifted her feet, lit another cigarette and looked down the street, exhaling the smoke with force.

"Strange? How?" Freya asked.

"Well, not the regular three letters and three numbers. Maybe personalized?" Lerlene looked questioningly at Martha.

"Oh, I know which one you mean," Martha chuffed. "All it said was BRA 4."

"Are you sure?" Freya was texting Bob in the DMV, wanting to get the details on that car.

"The letters? Yeah." Martha nodded and snorted. "I've hated that word since I grew these." She jostled her breasts.

"Thanks, girls. Let's hope we can catch him soon. You women don't deserve this."

Alan was coming around the block again. Freya waved bye as she slid into the passenger seat.

"We may have a lead. Hoping to hear from Bob," she told Alan. Just then Bob texted back with a cryptic message: *Can't touch it. Protected info.*

"Shit! Take us home, Alan. We need to talk with the Captain."

She gave Alan everything the girls had told her. "Why can't we get the info? What does 'protected' mean?"

"I know someone on the paper. Maybe she knows what plates like that mean," he suggested as he drove back to the station.

Freya talked with the Sergeant and then stormed into the Captain's office. "Sorry, F, but I don't have the authority to open that can. I can ask the Commissioner, but don't hold your breath."

"Do I have to wait till the next girl shows up cut to pieces? Do we need another victim before we stop him? How many shall we let him grab off the street? This isn't London in the 1800s. Now we have the effing technology and still we can't get the effing perp!"

When Freya stopped her rant, the Captain's chair had rolled backwards under the force of her shouts. He was pressed against the opposite wall, gasping for breath.

"Sorry, Cap. Got carried away, there. Won't happen again." She brushed the lapels of his jacket and turned to leave the room. "But I'll find him one way or another," she promised before shutting the door behind her.

Alan was leaning against the car, grinning. "Heard you all the way out here. Anyway, I got something. The Brazilian embassy uses those letters. But the plates can move from car to car."

Freya sighed. "Who do we know at the Brazilian or any other embassy? Which embassies are around there? Let's take a look."

Leaving their beat, they headed for downtown, the posh section. Circling Embassy Row, Freya saw that the Brazilian embassy was across the street from the Norwegian embassy.

"This is almost too easy," she murmured while texting

Frigg, her sister. *Who do we know at the N embassy?*

Dunno, Frigg texted back, *Ask Thor*. And so it went. Finally, she had her answer. "You don't say," she mumbled.

"What you got?" Alan asked.

"A trip down memory lane," she answered while sending one more text.

"A good trip?"

"Meh," she answered, tapping her fingernails against the dashboard, waiting for her husband, Odr, to answer. *Talk to me,* he texted.

That was not the warm fuzzy she had hoped to get from her husband. On the other hand, she and Odr had a long history of cooling off periods after intense sessions of hot, unbridled, soul-burning passion. The tiny bouncing balls, telling her he was still typing, kept her eyes glued to the small screen. The typing stopped. Her phone rang.

"Hey, sweetheart," his familiar voice purred in her ear. "Long time no see. You miss me?"

"Cute, O. How are the kids?"

"Beats me." He laughed. "They were fully grown when born and never listened to either one of us. What can I do for you? Need me to beat up someone?"

"Funny, as if I can't take care of that myself. No, I need you to give me some info."

"Like what?"

"I'm on a case that might involve one of your neighbors across the street. Know anyone who drives a car with BRA plates?"

He laughed. "Sure, all the top people have diplomatic plates and the rest borrow the cars when they can. Why don't you stop by and we can chat without anyone listening in."

"Are you at the office?"

"Yeah."

"We're parked out front. Tell your man at the gate to let us in."

Ten minutes later, Freya and Alan were comfortable, sipping coffee in Odr's office.

"That's why we're here," Freya said after she'd filled Odr in on what they knew. "We need to know who was driving that car last Friday. He could be the one we need."

"Follow me," he said and led them to a room in the basement. "We have cameras everywhere. And I'm sure our neighbors are watching us as well. Let's take a look at last week's footage."

"There!" Alan pointed to a grainy shot of a man in a trench coat walking to a row of parked cars.

"Can you get an enhanced shot of that?" Odr asked the technician.

"I'll try, sir," she said. "That's as good as I can do, sir," she stated after a few adjustments.

"Do you know him?" Odr asked the young lady.

"I believe his name is Juan, maybe Juan Carlos, sir. I think Anika knows him better."

"I see." Odr scratched his beard and nodded.

The young woman smiled. "One moment, sir." She stepped out of the small room.

"So ..." Odr turned to Freya. "Want to have dinner?"

"Yes, let's." She blushed and cursed her fair complexion and the effect he still had on her.

Alan rolled his eyes and, while focused on the screen, he toggled a switch and watched the footage roll on. While Freya and Odr were grinning at each other, Alan noted the license plate of the car that left the compound. He fast-forwarded through the tape and took note when the car came back.

"Frey." He nudged her. "Look." The man in the trench coat got out of the car and walked back into the embassy. "Does he have stains on his coat? What do you think? Could that be blood?"

"I think so, yes," Freya said.

"Shall we go over and chat?" Alan suggested.

"No can do, man." Odr shook his head. "That's not US soil. This is not US soil." He pointed to the floor in the small security room.

"Oh, right. Of course." Alan and Freya looked at each other, realizing there would be more to the case than simply finding the guy.

The security technician came back in and handed Odr a piece of paper. "Thank you, Gizelle," he said, giving her his most charming smile.

She blushed. "You are welcome, sir."

"Let's go back upstairs and have another drink." Odr ushered his two guests from the small space. Back in his sitting room, he explained the tricky situation. "I can, by invitation, go to the Embassy, but I cannot knock on the door and ask for a cup of sugar. You two, as law enforcement, cannot knock on the door and expect to be invited in. And even if you are, you have no jurisdiction once inside."

Freya and Alan nodded. "So, we need to catch him out on the street."

"Partially true," Odr agreed. "But if one of my employees is caught breaking the law on US soil, that employee would be sent home folded up in the next diplomatic pouch and the law here would never see him or her again," Odr explained. "Now when shall we go to dinner? I know a lovely place. A bit off the beaten track. Not the best neighborhood. But excellent Chinese."

"Oh?" Freya raised her eyebrows. "Where would that restaurant be?"

"Beijing." Odr grinned.

\#

That night, while she paced up and down the sidewalk, Freya smiled, remembering their lovely dinner date. It had been years since she had seen Odr. He never failed to live up to his reputation of inspiring longing and passion. But it was his anger and temper that made him so difficult to live with. Though, if she was honest, as the goddess of war, they had been well matched in the temper and passion department.

A car drove by slowly and stopped in front of her. She bent at the waist to look in the open side window and frowned. "What are you doing here?" she asked Odr, who was grinning at her.

"I was driving around, seeing if there was any real estate for sale around here. Picture my surprise when I see my wife, the incomparable goddess of love and sex, standing on a street corner. Such an open invitation to anyone ..." He tut-tutted. "I could make you an offer you couldn't, and never have, refused." He waggled his eyebrows. "Or we could circle the blocks and discuss how I could help you."

"Tell me what was on that paper Gizelle gave you last week, Odr," Freya asked for the dozenth time, pinning him down with her eyes.

"The man you're looking for is known." Odr sighed. "He has been stationed at various embassies and gets moved around a lot. Rumors and innuendos aplenty, but nothing ever sticks." Odr shrugged. "His daddy has more than one finger in the political pie back home."

Freya leaned on the doorframe and thought aloud. "So, a slap on the wrist, a tsk-tsk, don't do that again, is not going to work, is it?" Freya understood.

"Probably not. Let me help, Frey." A spark of anger and excitement flamed in his eyes.

"Head's up." Alan's voice cracked through her ear piece. "Champagne-colored, four-door sedan turning the corner."

"Move on, Od." She straightened up and stepped back from his car. Odr pulled away slowly.

The light-colored sedan pulled up. The window smoothly slid down. "How much?"

"What do you have in mind?" she asked.

"Don't be coy. A hundred, take it or leave it," was the curt answer.

"Bossy much!" She laughed, opened the car door, and slid inside. "What's your name, hon?" she flirted.

"Never mind my name," he hissed

They rolled away and turned a corner. The man kept looking in the mirror. After a few blocks, he cursed and sped up. Two blocks, three, weaving around slower cars, screeching around corners.

"What the …!" she exclaimed, clutching the dashboard.

"Shut up. We're being followed," he said through clenched teeth.

"Well, let me out," she protested, but she knew that he would not take the chance of slowing down.

"Where are you taking me?" she asked, hoping to give Alan the intel, but she didn't get an answer.

After a twenty-minute harrowing ride down a dark B-road, he turned into a driveway and rammed through a flimsy metal and chicken wire gate. The man stopped the car abruptly, took Freya's wrist and dragged her across the bench seat out of the car. Running around the back of the building, he pulled a knife from a pocket.

"Whoa, man!" she protested when she saw the knife and raised her arm to deflect it away from her face. She hissed when the sharp blade sliced into her forearm, unleashing her anger. She forced herself to relax and let him push her against the wall. The sudden lack of resistance pulled him off balance just enough for her knee to connect painfully with his balls. He groaned, dropped the knife, and bent at the waist, instinctively trying to protect his privates after the fact. Freya, whose anger made her grow taller and stronger, took the opportunity and slammed her fist under his jaw.

He staggered back, sank through his knees, and kneeled at her feet. When he grappled for his knife, she set her stiletto on the back of his hand. He cursed. "Get off me, bitch!" he demanded

"Oh, no. You don't get to call the shots!" she exclaimed. "You cut me! You think you can just spill my blood and walk away?"

She grabbed his hair and made him look at her. "Why? Why do you slice up women?"

Through clenched teeth he growled at her. "I like it. I like cutting pretty things and making them ugly. And you putas deserve to be ugly."

"Why?" She was puzzled.

"My father liked pretty putas better than he liked me or my mother. All of you need to pay."

"And the little boy in you, who is still crying for his daddy, is not going to stop. Are you?" She shook his head and used her special talent to see into the future. A long trail of pain and destruction stretched out before her.

His scoff of derision told her enough.

"Right." She nodded. "Since you injured me, I am now defending myself the best way little ole me can. You see, I am just a weak woman who's panicking. The adrenalin flowing through my veins is impairing my judgement. I just don't know my own strength. And once I've started, I can't seem to stop myself," she explained, smiling calmly while she grew another few inches. She wrapped her hand around his throat, pulling him up till he dangled a few inches above the ground.

"Oh dear." She clicked her tongue. "You are getting a little red in the face." She tilted her head and squeezed a little harder. "Breathing is not so easy now, is it? Tell you what, I'll let you have one more breath. One chance to say you are sorry." She eased up on the pressure against his windpipe.

"You vadia—" was all she allowed him.

"Yes, I thought so." She nodded.

"How long are you going to toy with him, dear?" Odr was leaning against the wall, a few feet away. "I thought we could go to dinner when you're done here. I was thinking of a lovely picnic on the Swollen River. Bet we could make that barge rock again. You do remember, don't you, little girl?"

She looked down at him from her anger-induced, seven foot height and chuckled.

"Yes, love. I remember. That would be lovely." She nodded. "But let's do that tomorrow, shall we? I'll have a mountain of paperwork tonight. But should be off duty for a while, pending the internal investigation." She blew him a kiss. "You may want to leave now. Plausible deniability, DNA, and all that."

He chuckled. "Sure, holler if you need me. I'll call you." She nodded as she watched him walk away. She'd heard those words many times before.

Minutes later, she sighed. "Oh, no. Look, he cut me. Ouch. And see what he made me do."

Alan took pictures of her wound and the body that was crumpled on the ground before calling their back-up and the CSI team.

\#

Freya's two black cats pulled her chariot at a leisurely pace while crossing the Rainbow Bridge into Folkvangr, her home. Odr, while lavishing her neck with kisses, whispered, "I wonder if you could make a habit of killing mortals. See how pleasurable the time between can be?"

She purred her agreement.

Source: Wolf Grove Media LLC – Anthology Submission

Dora The Explorer

"Are you really going to do this?" Rebecca looks at her with big eyes. "Nobody has ever done it. Are you sure?"

"If I want to have my name in books, then yes I need to do something nobody else has ever done. I can't just repeat climbing the same mountain many other people have climbed. People will say, 'Sure, well done, kid.' Then they'll pat me on the head and move on. I'd just be an arm note. One of a few women to have done it."

"Don't you mean anecdote? And you'd be the youngest. That should count for something, right?"

"Yeah, sure. Until someone even younger comes along. No. If I want to be famous I need to do something new, daring, groundbreaking."

"Or water breaking."

"Right! Exactly. Water breaking."

The two girls, Dora age seven and a half and Rebecca age six and three-fourths, trudge on. They drag a clothes line behind them. Rebecca holds a small grocery bag, which has a candy bar and two water wings.

"You didn't bring me a candy bar?" Rebecca is rooting through the bag but doesn't find another one.

"Am I supposed to feed you too? Isn't it enough that I'll give you credit as my coach, trainer, and moral support person?"

"Well, do you know how to spell my name?"

"I think so, yeah. But my editor may get it wrong. Then it's out of my hands."

"Still … You could have brought a candy bar for me too."

"Why didn't you think of your own candy bar?"

"I didn't, okay! I didn't know we were going to do this today, alright? I thought I'd get to go home and have tea with cookies and little tea sandwiches. My mum makes the loveliest tea sandwiches. She cuts the crust off and slices the cucumber really thin."

"Ugh! Cuke's. Sounds like puke. Nah, I'll take a peanut butter sandwich anytime."

"I wouldn't know. Never had one. How much further?"

"Another ten or twenty minutes. Over there is the nearest point. And as far as I can tell, the sea is shallow all the way."

On they walk, Rebecca still grumbling about not getting her own candy bar and missing tea with mum.

"Here. Now wrap this end of the rope once around this tree and then we'll tie the other end around my waist."

"Why do we need to wrap it around this tree?"

"I don't know, it's what I saw in a picture. I guess those guys knew what they were doing."

"So, someone has done this before?"

"They've tried. But …"

"Well … if they wrapped it around the tree and didn't get all the way to the edge, then maybe we need to do it without the tree. I can hold you, Dora. I'm strong. You know I'm stronger than you. Here, take your water wings."

"No, I've decided against using them. I mean, how dorky do I want to be, you know?"

"Did you bring a camera? I don't see one in the bag."

"Um, no. I forgot."

"Well then. No one will know if you wore water wings."

"Still …"

"Come to think of it, how will people know you did it?"

"You will tell them, of course."

"Hm, maybe. If I had a candy bar. I could."

"Oh, for Pete's sake, have the blasted candy bar! Just don't let go."

"Water wings? I won't tell."

"No. I'll go without. You got me, right? Don't let go!"

Dora checks the knot around her waist. Making sure it is snug. Carefully she steps off the dry land into the shallow water.

"Sure you don't want your water wings?"

"What explorer has ever worn water wings?" Dora throws the scathing answer over her shoulder as she gingerly steps forward. "I can swim and it's not that far." She hopes.

Inch by inch, Dora wades through the chilly water that is not yet reaching her knees. If the water rises another couple of inches, the hem of her school skirt will be wet. Never mind; it's just water. On she goes. Carefully sliding one foot in front of the other, shuffling along the bottom of the sea. She's becoming increasingly aware that, yes, this is the sea. Not a bathtub, jacuzzi, or swimming pool. Not even a lake. This is the sea, salty and cold. And it has a current. One that she can feel tug against the back of her calves.

Feeling a bit more insecure, she glances over her shoulder at Rebecca.

"Pay attention, Becca. Don't look at the clouds. Watch me."

"But that cloud over there looks like an elephant. See? Now it looks like an aardvark. And that one is a turtle. A giant turtle. See? Oh, now it's a slug."

"You're just trying to frighten me. Stop it!" For it was working.

The pull of the water is a lot stronger than she thought it would be. She reminds herself to just keep shuffling, keep going forward. Not that the current is giving her much choice.

Suddenly the bottom gives way. Her feet have nothing to stand on and under she goes. Immediately she feels the strong current wanting to drag her forward. She gasps. Wishing she had her water wings, she struggles to the surface and coughs up salty water.

"Dora! Dora! Are you okay?" She hears Rebecca shout. "I can't hold you. I feel funny. Come back!"

"I can't!" But she's not sure if Rebecca can hear her. The sound of the surf is louder. She swims with all her might against the current, but there is no way she can overcome its pull. Defeated, she turns and lets herself be dragged to the edge.

"Becca! Becca! Help!" The water pulls her along. All she can do is keep her head above water and breathe. The target is coming closer and closer.

And then she's there. At the edge of the world. Her hands reach out as she screams, but something stops her. There is a ridge. Stunned, Dora feels around the edge. It's a glass wall. She's seen those in pictures of fancy hotels. They call those pools "infinity pools". She laughs.

Her body is plastered against the glass, and her hands grip the edge as she carefully looks over the rim. There, far below, barely visible through the sheath of water cascading over the edge, are four elephants, holding up the Disc, standing on the back of a giant turtle which slowly crawls through infinity.

"I did it! Rebecca, I did it!" Triumphantly, Dora tears her eyes away from the origin of her world and looks at Rebecca, who is struggling with her own problem: her hitherto unknown sensitivity to chocolate.

"Oh."

Source: Reedsy, December 10, 2024

Trudy: This one is for Jed. :-)

Duck Pond

The first time I visited Mom after she moved into her independent living apartment, I was pleasantly surprised. Her one-bedroom unit had everything she needed, including a washer and dryer and a minuscule kitchen. Yes, she'd had to give up some of her furniture, but what she had left fit wonderfully.

The feature that impressed me the most was the balcony overlooking the charming duck pond. The weather was lovely that week, and we sat out there soaking up the afternoon sun and watching seniors and little kids alike delight in feeding the cheeky white ducks. Those waddling, quacking critters knew who to intimidate and who to ignore.

Mom said that just a week before, there had been ducklings. Cute little yellow fuzz balls that followed the mother duck. But either they had grown up or the heron had decimated the duck population. We observed a moment of silence.

Then I announced that in my next life, I want to come back as one of those ducks. Placidly floating on the small pond, accosting unsuspecting toddlers, and startling seniors pushing their walkers and rollators, shamelessly begging for bread.

Mom said, "Hmpf." She was used to my fanciful declarations.

Two days later, she sent me to the store for milk and eggs.

Sure, it was a little overcast when I walked to the store, but I had not counted on the shower on the way home.

Undeterred, I walked on, repeating, "I'm practicing for my next life. I'm practicing…"

Source: Beta Reader

Five Against The Wind

Hello, copy desk? What's your name, kid? --- Phillip, are you ready to take this down?

Tuesday, January 30, 1940.

Leeuwarden, Friesland, The Netherlands. 23:34.

In the early hours, more than 3,000 competitors and amateurs anxiously waited in the dark at the starting point of the Elfstedentocht (Eleven Cities Tour). A 199 km skating race over frozen canals, rivers, and lakes that connect eleven historical towns in Friesland, one of the two most northern provinces in The Netherlands.

Yes, I'll wait. --- Can I go on?

Only when the Elfstedentocht Association determines that the ice is at least 15 cm thick throughout the course, will the race occur. The first of these races took place in 1909. Today was the seventh time the race was held. Only those who are members of the Association are eligible to compete, but anyone can participate.

This morning the conditions were less than ideal. The temperature was -15C, and the near gale force wind from the north-east did not let up all day.

Sure. Let me know when you are ready. It's not my dime. --- Right.

At 05:00, the starting gun sounded for the competitors. The amateurs left thirty minutes later. The veterans knew to wear newspapers against their skin to hold in their body temperature, but even that might not have been enough today. A small group of ten or twelve pulled away quickly. As soon as the skaters were away from the city, the full impact of the freezing wind was felt. It followed them as they headed south to Sneek, the first of the check points where each competitor must have his card stamped.

The water near the dairy plant in Sneek was still open. Normally the skaters would be klunen; I will spell: K-L-U-N-E-N. This means walking in their skates over any surface other than ice, like snow or carpet, to the nearest frozen canal. Or they can unlace their skates and walk in their shoes. This year the Sneek fire department had flooded streets, so they skated to the reentry point.

Damn! --- Hello? Copy desk? Get me Phillip, will ya? --- How much of that did you get? --- Right, fire department. Okay, here goes.

On they went via Ijlst to Sloten. After leaving Sloten, the course turned west to Staveren, and the wind became a factor. The strong, north-eastern wind constantly blew a fine mist of snow across their path, and staying in the center of the canal became work. The sun briefly appeared, bathing the vast, flat land in an ethereal golden light, but soon the sky turned grey again.

Blasted! --- Come on. ---Hello? Phillip? Good man. --- How far back? --- Right. Ready?

The first six skaters that passed the check point in Stavern were Piet Keyzer, Cor Jongert, Auke Adema, Sjoeke Westra, Dirk van der Duim, and Gerrit Gijzelen.

--- What? --- Yes, I'll spell that for you later.

The men warmed up with hot chocolate before turning north to Hindeloopen via Workum. The wind was now square against them. Sometimes they would come to a standstill, but eventually they reached Workum.

Spectators braved the cold to cheer on the skaters. The small group of men crouched down, trying to make themselves as small a target as possible. There were still many kilometers to go. Too early to fight for position, they worked together, skating in line. Every hundred strokes or so, the front skater would drift to the rear to take advantage of the slip stream.

They reached Busward, the halfway point, by mid-morning. Some were disgruntled to see that they were well off whatever pace they had planned since the wind and the cold had slowed them down. While gulping a cup of pea soup, they eyed each other warily, trying to take their measure. Who looked more tired? Who would be more likely to take off too fast, and who would fall back? How long could they work together before it would be each man for himself?

Yes, I'll wait. --- Ready? --- Come on, man. --- Okay?

After Busward, the wind came from their right again, but the 17 km leg to Harlingen wound mostly through the woods. The trees broke some of the biting wind. Many bridges in Harlingen were too low over the canals to skate under. The men had to lie on a skit and were then pulled under the bridges.

The course turned north-northeast after Harlingen,

directly into the wind again for 12 hard kilometers to Franeker. Snow began falling in earnest, covering the ice. Citizens tirelessly swept the lane. The top group was down to five men. Mr. Gijzelen had fallen away from the pack. His skate laces had frozen and snapped. The time it took to relace his wooden skates left him too far behind.

Their breaths froze on their skin as they exhaled. Icicles drooped from lower lips and chins and clung to scarves and sweaters. Around noon, the five checked in at Franeker. The snow now created white-out conditions.

Not again! --- Hello? Find Phillip for me. --- Yeah, I know. --- Ready?

The leg to Dokkum was the longest: 26 km northeast, followed by 19 km due north. They battled the wind, cold, snow, and fatigue. Though more volunteers worked to sweep the path, for more than 20 km the skating lane was too narrow for anything more than single file. They had to shorten their strides, slowing the pace even more. At this point there was no competition, just survival.

The rest of the skaters were too far behind to be of consequence to the outcome.

At 15:00, more than two hours behind the previous race in '33, the five forerunners arrived at The Drost Tavern in Dokkum, the last check point before the finish line. Here the five men made a pact. Cor Jongert convinced his fellow competitors to continue to work together.

Yes, you heard that right. He claimed that the last race, the one in 1933, had two winners.

Yes, I'll get you those names later.

Why couldn't they award five winners this year? Jongert argued, adding that they might well be the only ones finishing. They shook hands on the pact and set off for Leeuwarden. However, about 5 km from the finish line Auke Adema sprinted forward. The other four went after him.

Chaos ensued.

At 16:33 Auke was the first one in sight of the finish line. The spectators who had been waiting for most of the afternoon in the freezing cold broke away from the sides and clogged the last few meters. Auke was caught up in the enthusiastic melee.

At 16:34 Piet Keyzer crossed the finish line first but was also waylaid by the crowd.

Cor Jongert was the first to have his card stamped at the end point.

When the five men were introduced to the Prince Consort Bernhart, the prince suggested that all five be awarded the gold medal.

To recap.

3,404 skaters set off this morning at 05:00 on a 199 km race. Of the 688 competitors, 124 finished the race. The first skaters came in after 11 hours and 34 minutes. Of the 2,716 amateurs, 27 finished the course. The rest abandoned the ordeal, some with broken bones, many with frostbite or damaged corneas from snow blindness.

That concludes my report. Thank you, Phillip.

Source: Reedsy, January 10, 2025

Flight Out

When I was sipping my black coffee, I realized that Bill had not eaten dinner last night and had not ordered breakfast.

"Wait. Didn't I see your obit last week?"

"Yes, you did."

"Madame. Plus de café?" Jean asked, holding the coffee carafe.

"Non, merci." I smiled. The seat next to me was empty.

Source: Blue Marble Storytellers Forum

Give Peace A Chance

"Careful now." I cringe the moment the words leave my mouth. Even though her back is toward me, I know my granddaughter Julie is rolling her eyes. Can't say I blame her. Sometimes I forget that not everybody has difficulty seeing and moving, let alone negotiating a simple stepladder.

The box she's reaching for falls apart at the first touch. A shower of papers and dust flutters to the floor of the closet.

"Oh dear." I sigh, thinking of the mess we just made rather than the value of anything that was in the box.

"Leave it, Nana," Julie says, hopping down from the ladder. "I'll get it."

She gathers the papers and hands them to me. My high school diploma in a cardboard tube no one has ever looked inside of in over 55 years, including me. For all I know it's empty. A few photos of our Junior and Senior year volleyball and softball teams.

"We had a perfect record those years." I smile as I show Julie the picture. "Zero wins. But the biggest and loudest audience." I chuckle. After all, who doesn't love the Keystone Kops?

The last photo is of me and one of my classmates, Marcelien. We are sitting on the floor in some hallway, sharing an orange Fanta. I can't remember where or when the picture was taken and turn it over to read the faded ink.

Marcelien – Hilton Hotel – 27 March, 1969.

"What does that mean?" Julie is looking over my shoulder.

"Did I ever tell you about the time I went to meet John Lennon?" I ask her.

"The Beatle?"

It's my turn to roll my eyes. As if there was another. "Sit down, I'll tell you."

Marcelien and I met in music class at the beginning of our Junior year. She was a brash, opinionated redhead who was never in doubt. Her burning desire was to become a jazz singer, and she confessed to smoking half a pack a week to lower her voice. Our music teacher tried to instill an understanding and maybe even a love for Bach and Berlioz, but we begged to sing every chance we got. After the first time we sang—*Greensleeves*, I believe it was—Marcelien leaned toward me and hissed from the corner of her mouth.

"From now on, just mime. I'll sing for both of us."

"She didn't!" Julie gasps.

I chuckle. "Yes, she did."

That was the beginning of our friendship and the second to last time I sang in public. The last time was a few years later, when I sang along with the radio, and my dog, who loved me, sighed meaningfully and left the room.

"No way!" Julie laughed.

"Yes, way." I sigh. I'm resigned to sing only in the car with the windows rolled up.

Those days, I rarely paid attention to the evening news. Dad would fall asleep and snore as soon as the anchor began to talk about the conflict between the Soviets and China and how many people had died in Viet Nam. So, I usually left the room. That's why I didn't know this bit of news till the next morning. While Dad read one of the inside pages of the Telegraaf, I leisurely scanned the headlines on page one.

The picture of John Lennon and Yoko Ono in bed looked interesting. According to the article, they were spending the week in bed at the Amsterdam Hilton to draw attention to world peace. My interest sharpened. I would have read the whole article, but Dad wouldn't give up the paper. I couldn't figure out, though, how they could achieve world peace by staying in bed for a week. But I assumed they had thoroughly studied the issue.

That day the halls at school were buzzing with the news.

"Let's go see them!" Marcelien said when we met up between classes. "It's half day. Let's go right after class."

"What's half day?" Julie asks.

"We had Wednesday afternoons free but had Saturday morning classes."

"You went to school on Saturdays?" She shakes her head at the foreign concept. I nod and continue.

"Today? I can't. I promised Mom I'd go with her to see my grandparents."

"Tomorrow then." She was undeterred.

"Yeah, right." I scoffed. "Tomorrow is a full day. There won't be enough time after classes to get to Amsterdam and be back for supper."

"There will be when we cut afternoon classes."

I must not have heard her right. Cut? I was 17 and never cut classes. I don't count missing most of third grade with unexplained but excused belly aches. Or the many times our dog would show up at recess and gamely let all the kids chase him until the bell rang. Then he'd sit down and patiently allow me or my brother to collar him and happily walk home with one of us.

But a planned skip? No, I never.

I did not sleep that night. I tossed, planned, thought, imagined, worried.

I'm gonna cut class—I'm gonna cut class—I'm…

"Come on, Nana. You really never cut?"

"I know, right?" I sigh. "Hard to believe, but true. Made up for it in college, though." I wink.

At lunch on Thursday, while most of the students went home to eat, the two of us walked to the train station. We giggled with nervous excitement the full 27 minutes to Amsterdam Central Station.

We walked up the Damrak, fighting the cold wind, and passed by the Royal Palace, numerous shops, and a few movie theatres. *Butch Cassidy and the Sundance Kid* had just come out. We promised ourselves to come back soon and see it.

By the time we reached the Hilton, we were breathless and chilled. Marcelien told the concierge that we were representing our school newspaper. Not that our school had a newspaper, but the man didn't seem to care one way or another. He simply rolled his eyes and sent us to the seventh floor.

"Your school didn't have a newspaper?"

I smile. "No. School was about classes, homework, and tests. No sports, except the very limited volleyball season we gloriously lost, and one field day, equally better left unmentioned, at the end of the year. No chess club or debating team. Thirty minutes after the last bell, the doors closed." I laugh when she shakes her head with disbelief.

Pandemonium, or possibly controlled chaos, greeted us when we stepped off the elevator. People scurried up and down the hall, leaned against walls, and lingered in doorways. Camera men and photographers cradled their equipment while discussing lenses, lightmeters, filters, and which new one they'd buy with the money from the marvelous shots they'd sell. Here and there groups of people sat on the floor, playing cards and telling tall stories.

Transistor radios, tuned to Radio Veronica, a ship in the North Sea, blared Marvin Gaye's *Grapevine*, The Who's brand-new *Pinball Wizard*, and Peter Sarstedt's *Where Do You Go To*.

Men, and even some women, were anxiously preening in front of mirrors, fluffing hair, powdering shiny noses, and smacking freshly glossed lips.

"Why did you say 'even some women'?"

"There weren't many women reporters or anchors in those days."

"Really."

I nod and continue.

Marcelien and I stood and stared. I was overwhelmed, ready to turn around and go home, but she had more staying power.

"Excuse me? Sorry? May I ask …? Excuse me?" Nobody stopped to give two teens any notice. Though Marcelien had dressed for the occasion in an orange and yellow pop-art dress that clashed gloriously with her red hair, our army surplus bookbags gave us away as mere school kids.

More people came off the elevators, shoving us aside. We let ourselves be swept down the hall until we stumbled over a boy our age.

"You told them you're here for your school paper, right?" His voice sounded groggy, as if he hadn't slept or had just woken up. He was using his Levi jacket as a pillow, and a small pile of garbage surrounded him. He clutched a half-empty bottle of Fanta.

"Yeah, so?" Marcelien asked him.

"Nah, 's cool. It just means you're at the end of the line. Been here since Tuesday evening. Came as soon as I saw it on the news. Might still be here on the weekend." He shrugged.

"Damn!" she mumbled and walked away to verify. Zander told me he was from Rijswijk and would probably be grounded for the rest of the year when he got home. "But if I get in to see them, it'll be totally worth it." He grinned.

In the end, Zander took this photo with my little Agfa. Despite all her bravado, Marcelien wasn't about to be late for supper either, so we wished Zander luck and walked back to the train station. We were back at the school building in time to blend in with the last of the students going home.

"So, you never did meet him?" Julie sounds disappointed and gets up to find the vacuum.

"No, we didn't." I wonder, though, if Zander ever made it to room 702.

Source: Beta Reader

Gone To The Dogs

The floor is sticky with pretzel crumbs fermenting in spilled beer. The air is heavy with cigarette smoke and resignation. Unfocused eyes try to see the good in what used to be. Restless fingers pick at scabs of old slights.

At the long bar, Jake stares at his track sheet. Herman misses the mind-numbing routine of work, and Michelle, though lonely, has given up on finding someone who'll listen to her stories.

I stare into the bottom of the glass and swirl the sweating tumbler over the scarred surface. When I drain the glass, the question will be whether to order another one or leave and go to where my ghosts wait.

Where memories of comfort food mock me. Where I reach in vain for cold feet to warm. Where private jokes, hugs, and secrets are no longer shared. Where smiles and laughter are history.

Where the nightmares of pain, shots, pills, and nausea linger. Where the bitter memories of brave but helpless smiles haunt. The place where promises were made and fanciful dreams were whispered, knowing time would run out.

Although I'm not ready to face my horrors, I shrug on my coat and turn toward the cold wind coming up the avenue.

Around the corner, a whimper comes from the dark alley behind the bar. The high-pitched nasal sound reminds me of Max, our lab when I was a kid. Using my phone's torch, I slowly enter the alley. Tied to the handle of the dumpster is a small dog. The rope has very little slack. It dances away from and snaps at rats. The rodents scurry when I shine the light on them.

I don't think. I act. Untying the rope from the container, I carry the trembling thing under my coat until I come to the all-night bodega two blocks from my home.

Clueless, I wonder what a little dog like this would eat. The woman working the late shift takes one look at the rescue. "Babies, soon," she predicts, nodding sagely, and sells me the expensive stuff.

The sky is fading to a nondescript grey as I sit at the small table in the kitchen. Thoughtfully, I swirl the coffee cup over the worn Formica surface. Underneath, snuggled on an old quilt, huddled near the radiator, are mother and two babies.

Can I move on and take care of another life? Do I have anything left in me to give? Wouldn't I be disloyal? What if I fail? How would I know what it needs?

A bump against my shin makes me look down.

"Hi, little mama, what do you need? You want another bite to eat? You bet. Tomorrow I'll see if I can find you a winter coat. Would that be okay?"

Source: Beta Reader

How I Ended Up In A Duck Pond

"Quack, quack, quack. Oh, shut up! Quack. Wait! That's me? Quack, quack. Quaaack! I didn't mean it. I was quack kidding."

NO, YOU WEREN'T.

"I was. Really, I was. Quack! Who are you?"

THE ONE WHO TOOK YOU ACROSS.

"Oh, quack. I'm dead?"

I often visited my mother and thought the best feature of her independent-living unit was the balcony overlooking the duck pond.

I enjoyed watching the raft float placidly on the water, patiently waiting for a child, clutching its mother's hand, offering stale bread. Then the team would become pushy and rude. And woe the senior citizen out for their afternoon walk, pushing a walker, having forgotten the bread. They would be chased by the full waddling for several yards, loudly accompanied by fowl name-calling.

"In my next life, I'm coming back as one of those ducks," I announced gleefully one afternoon.

"Hmpf," my mother said. She had heard my fanciful declarations before.

Two days later, she sent me to the store to replenish our G&T supplies. As I walked home, a pop-up thunderstorm caught me off guard. Having no choice, I continued, muttering my new mantra: "I'm practicing for my next life. I'm practicing for my next life."

I didn't feel the lightning.

SO, YOU REMEMBER YOUR WISH.

"But wishes don't quack true."

NOT FOR MOST. BUT YOU WERE VERY SINCERE AND THAT GLUED IT IN PLACE. HAVE A GOOD AFTERLIFE.

"No, wait! What do I do?"

FLOAT, WADDLE, WHATEVER. IT'LL COME TO YOU.

"Quack."

Source: Beta Reader

How I Found My Poise

I am about to run out of Poise, both the product and the attitude. So, I slip into my shoes, grab my keys, and make an emergency run to the store. To make the mad dash worth my while I reward myself with a bottle of wine.

When I approach the diaper aisle from the dairy section, I see him sneak in from the opposite end. Being curious, I watch him approach, assuming he'll stop at the small people diapers; he looks young enough. But he keeps walking and passes behind me. So, he is on his way to get milk, I conclude and forget about him till I realize he is standing next to me, perusing the men's version of Poise.

I side-eye him and smile wryly when I realize he is watching me.

"Our favorite aisle, right?" I smirk.

He blushes. "I'm new at this," he confesses.

"You realize that this is not the same as asking if the melon is ripe or what to do with artichokes, right?"

He looks stunned for a second then bursts out laughing. "Right." He snorts then sobers. "But why not?"

I lean against the shelves, cross my arms, and raise my eyebrows. "Anatomy."

He copies my stance and grins. "What about it?"

"Don't pass this around among your buddies, but girls and boys are made differently," I say.

He sucks in his lower lip, widens his eyes. "How?" he whispers.

I look behind me and make sure there is no one lurking behind his back. One more time over my shoulder then I make a circle with the index finger and thumb of my right hand and push my left index finger through the circle.

He laughs. It is my turn to blush.

"If I pay for that wine"—he nods toward the bottle in my basket—"will you cook dinner for me? Maybe you could teach me about the stuff I'm not to tell my buddies." He winks.

I consider this while I look him over. There is grey at the temples and more sprinkled among his dark hair. But his skin is still firm, maybe some softening around the jaw line. His laughing brown eyes have creases radiating from the edges, giving him an impish look. His six-foot frame looks firm, probably from regular visits to a gym. His worn jeans are molded on him, as is his t-shirt.

"Me, cook?" I feign horror while my heart speeds up and I hold my breath. It has been so long since anyone has flirted with me. It is a lovely spring-like afternoon, I remind myself, and I decide I am going to flirt right back and have fun. Just this one afternoon I will live as if it is 1999. Mentally I scoff; better suspend all reality and live as if it is 1994, or even further back.

"Okay." I straighten. "Let's go shopping."

In the parking lot I give him my address. Who am I? Why would I give a total, though cute and charming, stranger my address?

I chop, sauté, caramelize, reduce, add stuff to taste, and simmer. Then I take a shower. When I turn to the mirror I freeze.

Nu huh! No way!

I lean closer. No softly wrinkled skin, no interesting but tell tale grey streak in my hair, no droopy eyelids. And no, or at least barely noticeable, sagging body parts. As if I am forty-something again.

I am dreaming, right? This is not real, right?

But my make-up drawer still has make-up and my pill drawer is devoid of pills. My closet is full of clothes that are several sizes smaller and easily considered vintage.

Why am I not panicking? Why am I feeling excited?

I briefly, almost clinically, wonder where all my pull-on stretch jeans and XXL sweaters are. I reach for one of my old favorites, a red, slinky knit dress.

Then I turn back to the mirror. Yes, Mamma! My forties were wasted on me. I can do this!

As I walk by the window, I see a '92 corvette pull in the parking spot. I stop and watch for a minute till I see him climb out, a bemused smile on his face. He looks good, really good, in fitted jeans and a soft silk shirt under a long black coat. I decide not to take the ice cream out of the freezer. We might not get to that tonight.

"Hello." His eyes drag from my face down my body and back up as soon as I open the door. "You look … delicious."

"Thank you." We drink in the moment, knowing we are out of step with time, savoring this magic gift.

"Come in. Will you put on some music?" I point to the stereo that wasn't there earlier. "While I put the last touches to dinner."

"I will, in a minute," he murmurs as he dips his head and touches his lips to mine. Just a kiss, no other touch. A promise. With a shiver, I kiss him back.

I set the table, stir the sauce, and brown the veal. He stands close behind me, his hands lightly on my waist, sliding over my hips, pulling me closer. His breath skims over my neck, evoking a sensuous shudder.

"Pour the wine, please?" I pant, trying not to become too distracted and ruin our dinner at the last moment.

We sit across from each other, Seal serenading in the background. We talk and laugh about little things and nothing. Our fingers touch now and then, our eyes meet often, our feet play under the table. He refills our glasses but doesn't sit down after he puts the bottle back. He reaches for my hand, and we dance. Without words. Without jokes. Without overused compliments.

He holds me; I melt into him.

"Do you want coffee, dessert?" I whisper when the cd starts over again.

"No coffee. But for dessert ..." His voice trailed off to a warm breath ghosting across my cheek. Smiling, I lead him into the bedroom and close the door.

Source: Reedsy, January 13, 2025

I Want What She Is Having

Oh, this is ludicrous. She should leave. What possessed her to make that call? Battling with herself, fingers twisting painfully together, head and eyes down, she tries to blend into the background.

The door opens. Automatically, she looks.

He takes a quick look around the small restaurant and walks straight to her table, smiles, and introduces himself. Takes the chair near her when she nods, inviting him to sit down.

"Tell me. What can I do for you?"

Easily six feet, confident, casual, poised, he leans forward. His eyes, showing laugh lines, focus on her. His short hair has a hint of grey at the temples. A softening at the jaw, a quick disarming smile. It all adds up to a man utterly comfortable with who he is, what he does.

He waits patiently for her to answer his question.

Staring at her tightly woven fingers, she sucks in her lower lip and bites down.

The waitress startles her. He smiles at the young woman. "Two coffees, please." Returning his attention to her.

She exhales. "I don't think I can do this," she whispers. "It's too embarrassing. I'm sorry I dragged you out here. I'll pay for the full time, of course."

"Let's just have our coffee, then." A nod. "Tell me about yourself."

She huffs. "There isn't much to tell. Really, I'm quite ordinary."

Another nod. "Do you work?"

A shake of her head. "No. I'm retired." A shrug. "I like to read and have tried writing." A dismissive wave of a hand. "I just dabble. Short stories. They're just for me. I'm not looking to publish. Heck, I haven't even shown them to my friends."

He thanks the waitress with a smile when she places the cups on the table.

She takes a packet of sugar when he holds up the bowl. Declines the cream.

"What kind of stories?" he prompts.

"Ah, yes. Therein lies the rub." She smiles ruefully. He arches an eyebrow, encouraging her to continue.

"No, it's too …" She shakes her head. "I can't … It's not something I ever talk about."

She digs through her purse and places money on the table to pay for the coffee, reaches behind her, fumbles with her coat. He stands, helps her with the sleeves.

"Let's walk a little," he suggests. "There's a little park across the street with a pond. We can let the ducks chase us." He holds out his arm to her.

Despite her unease, she smiles and slips her arm under his elbow. As he predicted, a duck or two follow them but give up after a few yards. They pass a bench, a second one.

"I don't think I've ever had an orgasm," she blurts. "Fantasies, yes. But …" her voice fades. Without comment, he patiently walks next to her, waits for her to continue.

"Oh, I'm no virgin. Never kept count. But I read these so-called naughty books, you know? Not to brag, but I felt I could do better. Then I realized I don't know what they're talking about."

He makes a non committal sound, prompting her to continue.

"When I was eleven or so, my mother gave me a piece of paper. It was a letter that someone she knew had written and mimeographed. I'm really showing my age now, aren't I?" She laughs softly.

"My mother said to ask questions if I had any and then she left. Even before I read the letter I understood that this subject, menstruation, intercourse, procreation, and everything that goes with it, is not something nice people talk about. Ever."

She continues, "What I read that day was very clinical. There was nothing about fun, or pleasure. It really didn't sound like something I'd want to have anything to do with. Not the monthly mess or anything else. Maybe that's what the lady had intended." A shrug, a scoff. "Anyway, my mother was very relieved when I didn't ask questions. Oh, I had plenty. But …"

They circle the pond once more. She pauses as they pass the ducks, who ignore them in favor of a mother and toddler with bread.

"And yes, later I read those books that talk about owning my own orgasm and how sex was supposed to be joyful. But you know? If you don't know what 'it' is, if you don't know where 'there' is, and you don't know if you got 'there', how can you ask for 'it'?" Another pause.

"I've never been able to shake off that message, that nice girls don't say, ask, comment, or even are supposed to enjoy 'it'."

They walk on.

"To me it has always seemed to be messy, sweaty, and much ado about nothing, really. And to be honest, often painful. It was more like exercise." She shakes her head. "And I hate exercise." She huffs. "Lord! The number of times that I've wished he'd just be done and roll over, you know? 'Cause I do like cuddling and kissing."

She smiles.

She's silent for a while.

"The one message I learned, and learned well, is that it's taboo for me to talk about it. Taboo to ask to be touched here or there. Because, Lord forbid, what if I hurt his feelings? That would be the end of 'it', right?"

They circle the pond again.

"You know that scene from that movie, where the actress is faking an orgasm in a diner. You know the one? She was right, you know, many of us have learned to fake it. At least I have."

She sighs. "Oh, never mind. You've been kind to listen ..." Her voice trails off.

"Why stop now? Don't you think you deserve to know what real bliss is? Go ahead, say aloud what your fantasy is. Say all the things you've been taught to never say."

She sucks in her breath, looks around. "No, I couldn't. It's not right. I shouldn't … Really?"

He nods.

She is quiet for a while as they walk on. She takes a deep breath, but still her voice is shaky. "I want …" She pauses. "I want to know if those 'naughty' books are right. Is an orgasm really *une petite mort*? Just once I want to be 'devoured', be selfish, have it be all about me. I want what they're having. But …" She averts her eyes, shrugs.

"But?" he asks.

"Surely, you can see … Surely you know that my time has passed."

"Why?" He pulls her arm a little closer.

She shakes her head. "I'm old, grey, fat, soft, everything has gone south. I'd be too embarrassed, feel awkward. I …" She exhales. Her eyes are on the path, blinking rapidly.

They walk on in silence.

"Tell me," he encourages. "If you were writing a seduction scene, what would it look like? Where would it be?"

She giggles. For the first time since they left the coffee shop, she looks up at him. "Hah! A seduction scene?" Her smile makes her look younger. She's quiet for a few minutes as they walk.

"A yacht, I think," she answers thoughtfully. "Yes. At sunset. Soft music." A chuckle. "Al Jarreau or Barry White, something like that. Champagne, maybe. No, better make that something stronger." Another huff. A shrug. "Ach, it's all just a pipe dream, right?" she mumbles. "It'll never happen. Not anymore."

He smiles when he says goodbye at her car. "I enjoyed meeting you."

"Thank you for listening."

As she drives away, she thinks unburdening herself will probably be worth whatever his service will charge her. Two weeks later, assuming it's the bill from the escort service, she's surprised to find instead:

You are cordially invited on a sunset cruise.

Source: Beta Reader

Little Things

Yesterday, someone brushed past me in the produce aisle, leaving the scent of Joy behind. It was a little thing, but it transported me back 60 years to when I was uprooted and landed on Aunt Velma's doorstep.

I saw the small house at the end of the lane, tucked under the moss-draped trees. Heard the screech of a cicada as it broke through the breathless summer heat. Smelled the lilac competing with jasmine. I almost tasted the sharp-sweet tang of homemade lemonade and felt the ice cubes jostle as they settled in the glass.

When I suddenly needed a home in '64, the ones who lived there welcomed me with warmth and hugs. Their patience allowed me to grieve, their steadiness encouraged me to adapt, and their humor gave me room to grow.

"Lawd Almighty." With a sigh, Aunt Velma lifted the hem of her cotton house dress and let the fan blow underneath. The window unit had died in the middle of the night. Uncle Junior said he knew someone who knew someone who'd give him a good deal on another.

While we waited, the air grew heavier; movement, and even breathing, became a chore. The old fridge, like us, had difficulty doing its job. We'd put a pan with the last few ice cubes in front of the oscillating fan on the back porch. Aunt Velma said she'd seen it in a movie with Liz Taylor and Paul Newman. She admitted that it hadn't worked all that well for them either. But, she claimed, those two had been too angry to cool off. Today it was too hot to carry as much as a grudge.

I fished out two washcloths from the bucket of ice water, wrung them, and handed one to Aunt Velma. As we cooled our skin, we listened to the radio in the sitting room and hummed along with Johnny Cash's *It Ain't Me, Babe*. I would have preferred *I Want To Hold Your Hand*. But the AM station in Atlanta didn't reach this far.

A news bulletin interrupted the music: The bodies of the three civil rights workers, who had been missing since July 21, had been found on Old Jolly's Farm near Philadelphia, Mississippi. Aunt Velma sputtered her protests, murmured a curse at the violence.

"When will they stop? What are they afraid of? Fools, the lot of 'em." We sat in silence, wondering if anyone had learned anything. But we didn't have a clue. And more than 60 years later, I believe we still don't have a clue. Will we ever?

"What's keeping Junior?" she grumbled. "He's taking his good old time. Bet he's hanging around Arnold's, soaking up the cool air."

Aunt Velma always fretted when one of her chicks wasn't in the yard. It wasn't till years later that I learned to call her every week, knowing she'd imagine the worst.

I tossed the warm washcloth in the bucket and grabbed another.

"I remember the summer of '28." Aunt Velma's head rested against the high-backed chair; her eyes were closed.

"I was about as old as you are now. It was hot then too. But we were young, and the crick was still there beyond them trees." A vague gesture toward the bottom of the yard.

"Given half a chance, we'd spend the whole day in the water. Would have spent the night too, for it never seemed to cool much ..." Her voice trailed off. Either she was remembering or had fallen asleep. I left her to it and tried not to breathe.

"That's the summer Daddy left. Said living down here was a life sentence and he was due for parole." She lifted her hair off her neck, wiped her damp skin.

"Tommy and I figured he'd be back. Thought he'd miss Momma and us and come running home." A sigh and a slow shake of her head told me she still didn't believe the truth.

"Each day we'd ask, 'Has Daddy come back yet? When's Daddy coming home?' Momma just shrugged and turned back to the stove." Aunt Velma bit her bottom lip.

"We thought for sure he'd come back for Christmas, bring gifts. But he didn't." She fell silent again.

"Did he ever?" I asked.

"Did he ever what? Come back? No. Not then. It wasn't till ... I think it was the summer of '44, or maybe '45. Momma got word from the army that Daddy had passed. They brought him here." Aunt Velma nodded.

"We put him next to his mother and father. There among those trees." Her chin tipped toward the pine trees where the family plot was. There were no markers, but she knew.

"Later his brother Zachary joined them. And Momma a few years after that, and now Sissy, of course." She patted my hand. We both thought of my mother. I couldn't speak. Tried, but …

"Tommy is the one that's missing there." She coughed as she wrung out another washcloth and wiped her brow.

"Daddy had himself another family up there, some kids too."

"So, you went looking for them?" I asked. My voice sounded funny to me.

"No, not me … Tommy did after he moved up there. Said we have two halves. A half-sister and a half-brother. I'm trying to recall their names …" She paused. "Lucille, I think, was the girl's name. Which is kinda crazy when you think on it. Lucille was Momma's name."

"They never divorced, then?"

"Oh, no. Momma wouldn't hear of it. 'We's married in the eyes of the Lord. It ain't up to me to change that,' I heard her say. I reckon Daddy had asked at one time. I remember her railing to Aunt Phoebe that once. It's the only time I heard her raise her voice."

We let the cicadas have their say, ignoring a mosquito buzzing nearby while we hummed *Summertime* along with The Zombies singing on the radio.

"Did you know that Mother said y'all's Momma had chased her daddy away?" I asked. "She was so angry with your Momma." I tried to swallow my tears and anger, but I doubt I did.

Aunt Velma nodded, her hands lifted off the arm of the rocker—as close to a shrug as she'd do in the heat. Then she reached over and tapped my hand, resting her fingers on my knuckles.

"There are as many versions of the truth as there are people, child. We learn to create our own story as we understand it, and most of us don't go digging for more. Sissy was maybe four or five when our daddy left," Aunt Velma said, wiping the cold cloth behind her neck once again.

"When Momma didn't say nothing, Sissy must have made up her own story, I reckon." She paused, lifting her skirt again.

"Did he send money?"

"Daddy? Maybe once or twice. But no, Momma worked at the Jamison's and took in laundry on the side. Tommy found odd jobs the next year, when he turned twelve, and I had to help with the ironing. Lawd Almighty!"

She sighed again, watching me pour the last of the lemonade.

"Hated ironing ever since," she continued after taking a drink. "Had to use the stove to heat the irons when we couldn't afford power. I'd stand between the table and the hot stove and press endless yards of linen." She drained her lemonade.

"Momma changed after Daddy left," Aunt Velma added pensively. "As if part of her had gone with him. The fun part, the part that talked and laughed." A short shrug. "It always seemed to me that she was elsewhere, I don't know … And then Tommy went up there. She hardly ever spoke anymore after that." Aunt Velma's voice cracked before it faded.

"Where is that Junior?" Lifting her head, she looked toward town.

"How did you meet Uncle Junior?" I asked. I had heard the story before. It was a nice story and better than watching her worry.

"Church." She smiled. "A social, if I remember right. I think it was as hot then as it is now. And all of us in our Sunday's best, or what was left of them by then." She shrugged. This must have been in the mid-thirties; I understood what she meant.

"He was new in town. His family had just moved here from up north a ways. He walked right up to me after services. I can still see us standing under that big oak tree. Sissy and my friend Jolene and me. Remember the old tree they took down last year? That one. He walked up and said 'You's the prettiest girl here. I think I'll marry you.' I laughed at him." She chuckled.

"I was nineteen and didn't think I was a girl no more, you know?" She guffawed. "But he grew on me."

She smiled at me. I could feel her relax when we heard the rumble of a truck echo between the trees along the road.

"Well, finally." Aunt Velma sighed contentedly. "The slowpoke."

Uncle Junior's truck pulled into the drive, backfiring before coming to a stop. He grinned as he carried a large cooler up the back porch and dumped the ice in the freezer. He stopped and stole a kiss before walking back to the truck to retrieve a large, beat-up box.

Half an hour later, after his huffing and grumbling was replaced by the sputtering and rattling of the new window unit, he walked back onto the porch. We handed him a glass of fresh, cold lemonade. He drank it down greedily.

"Got a surprise for you, girl." His voice held a childlike sing-song tone while he carefully shut the door, hoping the small house would cool down enough by bedtime. Then he disappeared around the corner again. We heard the screech of the outside tap being turned on.

We giggled like schoolgirls when he set the sprinkler in the shade of one of the large oak trees. He stood within the spray's reach, head back, arms spread wide, grinning like a fool when the cool water hit him.

"Well? Come on, love. The water is fine," he teased. Aunt Velma got up and joined him; he held her while they kissed.

"Ain't you the clever one, Junior?" She sighed, leaning into him.

We arranged our chairs in the shade and let the sprinkler's mist cool us while we laughed at Uncle Junior's retelling of the gossip he had heard that day. Aunt Velma's smile erased the tension on her face. She leaned toward him when he spoke and her hand reached for mine, pulling me into her circle.

That day, more than 60 years ago, was Aunt Velma's 48th birthday and my 14th. We ate our cake at breakfast, convinced it would spoil in the heat. We have done so every year since. At the time, I was too young, too angry at the world, too occupied with my own loss to fully understand all the losses in hers.

In her subtle way, she told me that loss is part of life. But that one doesn't have to lose resilience and patience. It took years before I recognized her endless capacity for giving and loving. Now, anytime a little thing, like the scent of Joy, takes me back to that small house under the trees, I wish I could tell her thank you. Now that I understand better, I want to tell her I'm okay.

And I miss her.

Source: Beta Reader

(Love) Letter

Date: July 29, 2025

To: My old friend

Subject: Ghosted

Myths and folklore tell us that ghosts are immaterial. I will tell you that they have substance and emotions. We feel sadness, confusion, and anger. When you ghosted me, I lost trust and gained self-doubt.

I felt as if I had been tried, judged, and sentenced to solitary confinement without the benefit of accusations or the chance to defend myself. I was left to speculate what I had said or done that was so heinous that I had to be ruthlessly excised like a cancer.

Was I the only one who enjoyed our friendship? Did you see my enthusiasm as a desperate plea for attention? Did you interpret my joy as a sign of gratitude? Was I a pathetic nuisance and a burden? Did you lie each time you called me a friend?

Was I too blunt or too honest? Was I not helpful or supportive enough? Perhaps I was too self-absorbed. Did I not pay close enough attention to what you were saying? Did I misread what you said? Did I misinterpret what you shared? Or did I misunderstand what you meant? I never intended to be insensitive or ignore your feelings.

Should I apologize for having expressed my opinions and feelings? Should I have held my tongue? Am I wrong to believe that an honest exchange of thoughts and beliefs cannot damage a true friendship?

Was I oblivious to your protests whenever I hurt you? Did I not hear your protests when I overstepped your boundaries? And I'm sure I did; after all, I was human. Or did you swallow your irritation and hurt? Were you unable to tell me what you needed to say? And was it easier to callously throw away a friendship rather than confront me with my shortcomings?

I was surprised that you would rather turn your back than express your feelings. I would think that with your skill as a writer and your talent for creating thought-provoking prose, it would be easy for you to find the words to, if nothing else, say goodbye.

But now I know that the loss is yours, and I pity you and all the ones you will call friends and eventually discard because you are too cowardly to say what you ought to.

Your former friend.

Source: Beta Reader

Night Shift

Jack is two minutes late for work. Nothing unusual about that. He's actually ahead of his own schedule, just not his boss's schedule. He would have been on time, maybe even a minute or so early, if he hadn't knocked Mrs. Compton off her feet in his rush to leave home. Apologizing profusely, hauling her clumsily upright, and chasing and returning DeeDee, her toy poodle, had taken what little extra time he had allowed himself and then some.

Catching all the red lights was as normal as his toast landing peanut butter-side down.

With a grunt, he yanks on the employees-only door of the mega mart. The force pulls Mr. Zucker, the store manager, who was pushing from the other side, into Jack's arms, sending both men sprawling to the concrete.

"I'm sorry, Mr. Z. So sorry." Awkwardly, Jack lifts the skinny man to his feet. With a heavy hand, he tries to brush the dust off the manager's suit, only to end up spanking the older man's bony behind.

"Cease!" Mr. Zucker bellows. "Take your hands off me, you idiot!" Mr. Zucker shakes his head. "If it wasn't for your father … Never mind. It's a good thing you can't do much damage at night. Go! Go and try not to screw up."

"Yes, sir, Mr. Z." Jack drops his head. "I didn't mean to …" Mumbling apologies under his breath, he enters the dark building and fumbles with the payroll clock, accidentally clocking Amanada, one of the cashiers, in instead.

Hours later, Jack hums atonally while toying with his pencil. He doodles, erases, doodles, tries to twirl the stubby remnant between his fingers, drums it on the desk, taps it against his teeth, and throws it up to make it stick into the acoustic ceiling tiles. That last trick doesn't work. Luckily, it's the gnawed orange rubbery end that lands in his left eye, and not the pointy end.

With a curse, he sits up, rubbing his knuckles in his eyes. A useless attempt to substitute one pain with another but, in fact, doing nothing to relieve either pain.

What's that?

Something moves on the CCTV monitor. Nothing ever moves in the gloom of the cavernous store. Unless it's Jack himself getting another family-sized bag of Fritos and a liter of Diet Coke.

There!

Movement is picked up by one of the cameras. Whatever it is, it's fast, bigger than Mrs. Compton's toy poodle and smaller than Jack's father's pit bull. And why is it rushing up and down the aisles in the garden center? Excited over having something to do, Jack forgets about his dinner and runs the tape back and forward, back and forward in ever smaller increments till he realizes he can go frame by frame.

"Holy crap!"

Nobody will believe him. Not without a picture. He amazes himself and manages to print a still.

Remembering his dinner, Jack carries his bag of Fritos

with him as he hurries toward the garden center. Maybe it's the crunching as he eats one handful after another. Maybe it's the jingle of his keys—none of which fit in any lock—as he lumbers through the store. Maybe it's the very fact that he lumbers. But all is quiet when he stands among the flats of seedlings, bags of mulch, potting soil, and pesticides.

"Come on. I know you're in here."

Nothing, nada, zilch. Dejected, he returns to the relative comfort of his "office" after a much-needed detour through the snack and beverage aisles.

Tomorrow. He'll catch them tomorrow.

However, on Tuesday night, even though he uncharacteristically keeps his eyes glued to the monitors, there is no movement.

Wednesday night. Nothing

Thursday night. All's quiet. He keeps looking at the print, just to remind himself that he really saw it.

Friday night. Bingo!

He kind of jogs to the garden section. Again, he's too late.

Why does it come here? What does it want? Think, man. Think like one of those smart TV detectives. Better yet, think like a superhero. Has anything been moved? Is anything missing? Um … How can you tell if something is missing if you don't know what was there to begin with?

Deep in thought, he almost stumbles over a garden gnome that had been left out in the middle of the aisle.

"Sorry, little fellah," Jack apologizes to the little ceramic statue with a cute yellow floppy hat and carefully sets it with the other gnomes before heading back to the monitors. Again, he reviews the tape. Yes, there it is. A little gnome with a yellow hat, running around. How had it gotten away? It can't possibly be that fast. Can it?

Over the weekend, he can't think of anything but how to catch the little thing in action. Monday night, Jack takes a fold-up lounge chair from the sporting goods section, along with a small cooler, and settles in the garden center. He has enough Fritos, Coke and ice to last the night.

Nothing happens. At least nothing happens before he falls asleep around one-thirty.

Tuesday, he sleeps undisturbed through his shift.

On Wednesday, he wakes up when something tickles his nose. He tries but can't lift his arm to swipe the bug away.

"Huh?" He can't move. "What the …!"

His large, plump body is tied to the lounge chair with several garden hoses, the extra-long ones. On his chest, poking his nose with a thin, green plant stake, is a little man with a long white beard wearing, among others, a pointed red hat.

"What the f—?" Jack repeats. "Hey! I really did see you."

"No, you saw Dopey, there." The bearded man with the red hat sighs. "He's a green one and doesn't know how to be inconspicuous yet." The old man growls and adds, "You were not supposed to see him. You now will forget you ever saw him."

"Nah." Jack grins and shakes his head. "I'm afraid I can't

do that. You know, once you've seen a gnome, it sort of sticks with you." He shrugs, making the old man stumble. "Besides, I have pictures." Jack grins disarmingly.

"Hah, Marvin has already tampered with your CCTV get-up."

"You are too cute." Jack chuckles, making the little fellow bounce on his chest.

Indignantly, the miniature person plants his fists on his hips. "I am NOT cute. I'm over five hundred years old. I outgrew cute more than three centuries ago!"

"If you say so." Jack shrugs, toppling the old man. "Oops! Sorry about that. What are y'all doing here, anyway?"

The little man pulls himself to a sitting position. "We're garden gnomes," he explains. "We tend gardens. Normally we go to the Garden Center on the other side of town, but they are out of petunias. Mrs. Swanson has her heart set on petunias. Lord knows why. So, we had to come here. We'll just get them and be gone."

"Oh." Jack is disappointed. "And not come back?"

The old man shifts, moving off the fourth button on Jack's uniform shirt. He absentmindedly toys with a loose thread till the button pops off and ricochets against a fountain. "Oops." He chuckles. "No, we prefer the quality at the other place."

"How long will it take you to get back to Mrs. Swanson's?"

"With luck, the night after tomorrow. We'll over-day in the cemetery. Nobody ever comes there."

"I get off at six. Can get y'all there by six-thirty, easily. It'll still be dark. Of course, you'll have to let me up."

Something tickles at Jack's left ankle and then that knee. And on his other ankle. Pretty soon six gnomes have joined the bearded man on Jack's chest. And more are coming.

"Why?" the old man asks.

Trying not to shrug and still sound casual, he says, "Why not?"

"What's in it for you?" a gnome with a blue hat asks.

"Well …" Jack thinks. "What do you get out of doing Mrs. Swanson's garden?"

"Fried chicken," a little fellow with a yellow floppy hat pipes up and is promptly shushed.

"Dopey?" Jack cocks one eyebrow and stage-whispers to the old man, who sighs and nods.

"Well." Jack thinks some more. "Satisfaction. You know, the warm feeling you get, knowing you're doing something good. Something other than eating Fritos and runing into people." He starts to shrug, but ten pairs of small hands held up in consternation stop him.

"I don't know," the old-timer muses. "What do you all think?" he asks the other little men.

"Ride in a car, or haul two flats of petunias for two nights? We could even get a bag of mulch," one with a green hat says. Eight little pointed hats bop.

The old man stands up and sighs. "It goes against everything I've been taught, but alright. Let him up."

Jack exhales, sending seven hats flying. The smallest of

the gnomes is blown off its feet. Only the quick reaction of one of his mates keeps him from rolling off Jack's chest. "Oh, sorry! My bad."

Before the day shift shows up, the gnomes have carried two flats of petunias and one bag of mulch to Jack's car. Marvin has erased all the action from the CCTV feed and has shown Jack the new program, Gnomeface, he installed on Jack's phone. After he clocks out, Jack drives to Mrs. Swanson's home, where he drops off his new friends and their supplies.

"Call me next time you need a ride, okay?" He holds out one finger for a low-five.

Feeling good about himself, which, sadly, is quite unusual, Jack whistles as he drives home.

He is thrilled when Marvin texts him a week later.

M - **U free Sun?**

J - **U bet! 'sup?**

M - **Picnic?**

Slowly, cautiously, they form a friendship. First an occasional Sunday outing with just the small band of gnomes he met in the store. But soon other clans join. A lot of gnomes will fit in a Corolla.

The younger ones use Jack for climbing practice and then slide back down his chest and belly, doing flips and pikes and twists, giggling and whooping the whole way. Marvin patiently teaches Jack how to play the gnome version of Dungeons & Dragons. Others try to teach him the basics of gardening. But the latter isn't really his strong point.

Sometimes, before his shift, he'll run an errand with Graham, the old gnome, tucked in his chest pocket.

"You guys should have a business, you know."

"We have a business," Graham points out, gruffly. "We have been doing this for centuries."

"Yeah, I know, but … if you'd advertise. I don't know … have a warehouse, maybe. Your own greenhouses … Your own garden center …" Jack shrugs. "I mean, why use a middleman when you do it so much better?"

"Harumph." Graham is a hard sell, but eventually the younger ones convince the elders that, unlikely as it sounds, Jack may have a point. The next spring, a warehouse is rented and a greenhouse filled with plants and seedlings. Even though it's hard to believe, Jack is now the face, though not the brains, of a new landscaping service.

Enchanted Gardens.

Wake up to new beauty.

We work while you sleep.

For the first time in his life, Jack is part of a group, part of a family that accepts him with all his clumsiness, charm, awkwardness, cheer, and voracious appetite.

Source: Reedsy, June 18, 2024

Nuthin' Is Pretty Cool

Days ago, the young giant, too easily distracted, wandered away from his fellow giants. First, he loped after a butterfly. A pretty butterfly with many black lines and splotches of other colors. Until he got distracted by a skittish squirrel, but that little thing climbed higher up a tree than even the giant could reach. With a sigh of disappointment, the big guy moved on. He followed the spots of light that danced through the trees. Until those faded at the end of the day. That disappointment was also soon forgotten when he got a whiff of food—delicious meat, and other good stuff. There are very few things that will hold this giant's attention better than food.

He spent a few hours hunting through the garbage bags and eating all the tasty and smelly things he could find. Then he spent the night in a box, one that had fallen behind a dumpster. Each day he roamed, dividing his attention between what his nose found and anything that moved. Each evening, he found yet another pile of discarded food, and each morning, having slept in a box, he woke up as the birds started singing. Then he would set out to find those birds, only to be distracted by something else.

Little Lookie, on the other hand, hesitated before he left his yard. It was a good yard—a pretty yard with many toys but nobody to play with. When he heard his little neighbor leave, he slipped under the hedge and trailed Bobbie. Wouldn't it be great if the two of them could play ball, like they did a few days ago? Lookie knew that catching wasn't his strength, but he would tirelessly run after the ball and bring it back. Today, Lookie had hesitated too long, though. His little legs were too short to keep up with Bobbie. He didn't see his neighbor get in a van. And Bobbie never saw Lookie behind him.

Lookie whimpered at first when he lost sight of his friend. He kept running, though. Hoping he'd see or hear Bobbie so he could ask him to play ball. But Bobbie must have run even faster than normal. Lookie got himself all turned around, didn't recognize where he was. He knew he was in a park, but it wasn't the same one he had visited with his mama. He called out, hoping his mama could hear him. But she probably had the TV on, or maybe he was too far from home.

Aimlessly, he wandered through this new park. And though it wasn't the fantastic food his mama set before him every night, he was able to pull a few wrappers from a trash bin and put some food in his little tummy. Scared of all the strange sounds and shadows, he huddled under a park bench, shivering more from fear than cold, even though he wasn't wearing the coat his mama would make him wear when they went outside.

"What-cha doing under there?" the giant asked. His voice was loud, making Lookie quiver with even more fear.

"Trying to stay safe," the little fellow whispered.

"That's cool. You hungry?" The big one, who was always hungry, was lying on his belly, staring with curiosity at the miniature thing.

The little one nodded. "Very."

With a grunt and a huff, the giant stood up, towering over the undersized thing. He pushed against the trash bin, toppling it.

"Let's see what's for breakfast." He poked his enormous head into the bin. "Mostly snacks, but not bad," he declared. "C'mon. Take your share," the behemoth urged his tiny new friend. After all, the giant had only made friends and had never met a stranger.

"What's your name?" Lookie asked between licks, trying to clean the last of the goodness that used to be a Klondike bar.

"Don't know," the big one answered around a mouth full of cold hamburger, spitting out the pickle. "I don't think I own one. Do you have a name?"

"Yes. My mama calls me Lookie." The little fellow tried to unstick his tongue from the wrapper. "How about I call you Luke?"

"Luke." The giant nodded, happy to have something called a name. He nudged yesterday's cheese Danish toward his new friend. "Here, you need to grow."

"Thanks, but I think this is as big as I get."

"For real?" Luke looked at the undersized thing. "Wow. I think my Mom had kids bigger'n you." He paused for a moment. "I wonder where they are now."

"I miss my mama." Lookie stopped eating, having lost his appetite.

The worst of their hunger stilled, for now, they wandered

off. It wasn't necessary to learn chapter and verse about the other's life. It was great to have a friend to explore the park with, checking out each trash bin and finding a small creek to drink from.

Lookie soon fell behind. Luke's legs were so much longer, and he covered so much ground with just one step. Lookie's short legs just plum wore out trying to keep up.

"Can you go any slower?" Lookie puffed. "I'm a bit scared out here on my own," the little fellow admitted, "but I can't keep up with you."

Luke stopped and looked back, waiting for Lookie to catch up. "I don't think I can go slower. But you could climb on my back. Go ahead and try it." Luke flattened his belly to the ground, and Lookie scrambled up, grabbing hold of the rope necklace Luke was wearing.

"Ready?" Luke asked. Lookie grunted, concentrating on holding on to the rope. Carefully, Luke stood up and loped off toward the next garbage bin.

For several days, they crisscrossed the park and checked out the garbage piles behind the restaurants. The highlight of their buffet was the couple of dozen egg salad sandwiches. At night, while they shared the box, Lookie slept soundly, knowing the giant had his back.

Luke stopped in his tracks. The short hair on the back of his neck stood on end. That truck. His daddy had warned him about that truck. What had he said again? Run. Just run in the other direction whenever you see that truck.

So, he ran. Lookie lost his footing and slipped off the giant's back, but he was desperately hanging on to the piece of rope around Luke's neck. Alas, the little fellow had to let go; he couldn't hold on any longer.

Luke now had a decision to make. Was he going to keep running away from the truck or stick with his new buddy? The new buddy who had admitted to being scared on his own. Luke stopped and turned around. He found the little runt curled up in the grass, whimpering.

"You okay, man? Are you hurt?" Luke asked.

"I think so, I mean, no, not hurt." Lookie stood up and shook himself off. "Why'd you run, and why did you come back?"

"Duh!" Luke scoffed and looked a little sheepish—as if he does emotions. Hell, yes, he does! He nudged Lookie, toppling his little friend. His big ears picked up the sound of men running up the path, sensing that they were too close for Lookie to outrun them. Luke stood over his little pal. He'd defend him against whatever these men would want to do. Would they love them, or would they hate them? Would they kill them? He wished his dad had let him know.

The men stopped in their tracks as soon as they came around the corner. One of them hitched his pants up and pushed his mirrored sunglasses back in place.

"I'll be darned! What a pair. Hey, fellows, how about you come with us? Hey? We've got food, and we can probably find you a home. Wha'da-ya say, hey?" Slowly, the two men came closer to Luke and Lookie.

"You think they can find my mama?" Lookie asked.

"Don't know, buddy, but it might be worth a try. Just stand

still and let them do what they need to do, okay?"

"You're not coming?" Panic squeezed through his words. "Cause then I'm not either. You came back for me. I'll stick with you."

Luke sighed. "Okay, you're gonna be a hard case about it, aren't you? Sorry, dad. Alright. Together it is."

"Daryl wasn't kidding." Jason and Olivia, two volunteers at the animal shelter, stood back from the kennel, grinning, as they watched the gigantic dog, which they thought might be a cross between a Wolfhound and a Great Dane, sit in the corner of the kennel. The tiny Chihuahua was trembling, huddling between his front paws.

"What a pair. The little one has a chip. The owner is on her way. The big one doesn't." Jason shook his head. "Such a beautiful, friendly dog. Sure, he's a bit rambunctious, maybe not even full-grown. Someone had claimed him, but he must have chewed through the rope."

"Where's my baby boy?" Lookie's ears pricked up. He yapped at the sound of that voice, pranced on his hind legs, and scrabbled against the grill of the kennel. Luke wagged his tail. Happy for his little friend and trying not to think ahead. He rarely did anyway.

As soon as Jason opened the door of the kennel, Lookie rushed out, ran circles around his mama's ankles, then raced back in and nudged Luke forward. Come on! Come, say hello to our mama. Come on!

"She'll not have a big lug like me around. I'm nuthin'."

"She will, too! She's my mama. You're my brother. So,

she's your mama too." He gave Luke a quick bite on his hind paw. "And if you are nuthin', then nuthin' is pretty cool."

"Ouch, man! Okay, okay."

"Ma'am, is the big one yours, too?" Jason asked Marissa.

It took a minute to answer. She was laughing too hard watching Lookie yap and nip the big dog's neck while he rode the giant's back toward Marissa.

"I think he is now." She accepted a sloppy hello and scratched Luke behind his ear. "Hey, big boy."

Source: Reedsy, August 01, 2025

Pablo's Wisdom

It caught her eye, winked at her, made her fall in love. She just had to add it to her collection. Right there, on the modest table, among all the other market stands was the vase. A beautiful, ethereal pale green jade vase. She stopped and carefully, almost reverently, lifted it off the table, felt its weight, held it up to the light, and knew it was hers.

Exploring, traveling, learning about cultures different from her own, attempting to master at least a few words of the language, as well as seeing the sights and comparing architectural styles and art, had been ingrained. She had traveled with her parents since she was a small child. Learning had been encouraged and expected.

She loved her consulting job mainly because it involved much travel. Those trips hadn't always been roses and sunshine. There had been plenty of times when travel plans turned out to be just that: plans. Hype with not even a polite nod toward reality. Shifty drivers with rickety vans, ox carts instead of buses, barely clean hotels, dodgy food. Through it all she had learned to go with the flow, smile, and calculate how many dollars it would take to get her out of this pickle.

Photography wasn't really her thing. She didn't want to spend half her life behind a lens, preferring to absorb the sights, architecture, costumes, culture, and nature with her own eyes.

"When the time comes that I can't remember where I have been," she declared, often, "an old grainy photo won't help me, but a beautiful item, a piece of art, I will enjoy my whole life."

Wherever she was, she much preferred to walk around with her eyes open, taking in all she could see, smell, taste and touch. Always skipping the souvenir stores; nothing as gawdy as 'Greeting from Brighton' for her. She'd much rather explore antiques shops or artisans' ateliers. Maybe, now and then, she had been jibbed; maybe they, correctly, pegged her as a sightseer. She didn't concern herself with that. As long as she valued what she had bought, it didn't matter.

This long habit of bringing home at least one item, one artifact from each trip, had accumulated into a large, be it eclectic, collection of fine art and locally made pieces she felt were worth displaying. For instance, in Naples she'd found a miniature painting of Capri. The inlaid side table came from Mexico. The hand painted tiles in the kitchen back splash were from Greece. The crystal wine glasses had been bought in Prague. The exquisite amber necklace had come from Finland. The delicate soapstone sculpture had been made in Alaska. The silk shawl, shot with gold thread, had been hand loomed in India. She owned several pieces of opal jewelry she'd bought in Australia … And on and on.

On her most recent trip to Honshu, she had almost walked by the small stand in the market. Then she'd backed up and stared. Surely, she had never seen anything like this vase. The elegant shape, the exquisite color. It had to be one of a kind. When she picked it up, stroked the warm stone, she was sold.

She couldn't pass this up, could she? No, she couldn't.

Dutifully, she haggled with the shrewd vendor, though she was convinced she was robbing the old man. He carefully wrapped the vase in old newspaper and handed it to her.

Delighted with her unique find, she walked away. When she was well out of sight of the stall, the man reached under the table and put another, identical vase on display.

When she came home from her trip, she unpacked her treasures and carefully placed the vase in the middle of the low table in the center of the room. Each day when she came home, she would sit on her sofa and admire the vase.

Gradually she became aware that something was off.

It took weeks of experimenting. Placing the vase here, then there, up high, in this light or that corner. She added flowers, different greenery. Each time she put it back on her coffee table. She became more and more obsessed, trying to find the answer. How could one object she found so beautiful not fit in her room? Finally, she saw the answer. It was so obvious. How come she hadn't seen it before? The room simply didn't fit around the vase. The wall color clashed with the vase's unique shade of jade green.

The next day she contacted a painting service. "I want the walls to be the exact color of this vase," she explained.

"No problem, ma'am," the painter assured her.

The job, painting the one room, was finished in a few hours. When she came home from work, she called the painter. "It's not the right color. Please do it again."

"Yes, ma'am."

Four, five times the painter came back. Each time she

wasn't satisfied. Finally, the painter, utterly frustrated, at his wit's end, called Pablo.

"I know you're retired," he said by way of apology, "but your eye for color is unsurpassed. I've done everything I know to satisfy her demand, but there is no pleasing her. I know, I know. The client is always right, but … Could you please help me out and match the wall color to the blasted vase? I'm losing money on this one room."

"Sure." Pablo would never admit it, but he was getting bored sitting at home. Surely his wife could manage one morning without his supervision. "I'll be there tomorrow."

The next morning, she was waiting for him. "They say you'll be able to fix this problem for me."

"Yes, ma'am. I will." He unloaded his tools while she stood by and watched. Before he started to mix his paints, he turned to her.

"I was wondering, ma'am. Do you think you could get me a cup of coffee? I specifically like the coffee at that place on the other side of town. I don't know what they do to make it special, but it's unique," he enthused.

She shrugged. If he could make her room look just right, she'd go to Rio to get his coffee. Driving to the other side of town and back took her a little over an hour. When she finally returned with the cup of tepid coffee, Pablo had just finished and was washing his brushes and pans. While he loaded his supplies on the truck, she walked into the room, looked at the vase and the walls, then back to the vase, and smiled.

"You did it! You are a miracle worker. Oh, my! You are

worth every penny."

Pablo smiled, nodded, and, as soon as he had finished loading his truck, wished her a good day and drove off.

She gushed and praised Pablo to the painter who had recommended him.

Pablo's phone rang a little later in the day.

"Tell me, what is your secret?" the painter begged. "Whatever you did, she's ecstatic, can't say enough wonderful things about you. How in the world did you finally match the wall to that vase?"

"Well," Pablo answered thoughtfully. "Sometimes you have to paint the vase."

Source: Reedsy, July 19, 2024

Paradise Lost

(Paradise Found?)

I almost let the phone go to voicemail since I didn't recognize the number and suspected I would have to be rude to yet another salesperson.

"Yes?"

"Mr. Samuel Makarov?"

"Yes?"

"I have a story for you."

"Those are magic words. I'm a freelance reporter. I'll take whatever news I can get. Excluding who is sleeping with whom, who had a face lift or tummy tuck, or who got who pregnant. Talk to me."

"Not over the phone."

The man gave me the address of a coffee shop just out of town. We agreed to meet in thirty minutes.

Mr. Ahmed Sharuff, a middle-aged man, had a full beard sporting streaks of grey. His abaya and keffiyeh were simple, serviceable, and unadorned. Upon his urging, we strolled through the garden behind the coffee shop while he told his story. He said he made his living as a member of a salvage and clean-up crew. They specialized in cleaning up after bombings and explosions. He had not been without work in decades.

"Quite lucrative," he admitted with a shrug. "Officially, we're not supposed to take anything and bring it home. But you know

how it is. Normally I don't take anything, at least nothing big. But this time it was different." He shrugged again, holding both hands up in a helpless gesture.

"Something about this item spoke to me. It felt hot to the touch, much warmer than everything around it, yet comforting at the same time. I tucked it in my pocket. It fit as if it was made for it. We worked about a week longer at that site before we went home.

"As soon as I came home, the dreams started. They were both frightening and beautiful. Familiar and strange. Ethereal and normal. But, above all, urgent and compelling. Each night the message became clearer. Different voices, different languages, cajoling, demanding, feminine, musical, or fatherly."

The story Ahmed told me was interesting, but I was not convinced it was newsworthy. I pumped him for more information, asked for more evidence. He showed me pictures. Quoted phrases in languages he did not speak.

We met several times. He never wavered from his conviction and kept repeating that "This needs to be shared with the entire world. I was told to share this with the entire world. What if they bury it? They can, you know." He referred to the synagogue he had given the artifact to.

I followed up with the Jewish Great Synagogue. They confirmed that, yes, Mr. Sharuff had turned over the artifact. And that, yes, it was being studied.

So, I drafted his story and contacted an editor friend of mine, urging him to print it. It was ten days before he found enough column space between AI developments, wars, famine, and other general mayhem. Even then, the story was buried on page three.

Jerusalem Post

September 15, 2023

Recent Discovery.

Byline: Samuel Makarov, independent contributor.

This reporter was recently approached by Mr. Ahmed Sharuff, from Amman, Jordan. He informed that he had found a significant artifact while cleaning debris at an explosion site.

A series of low- to mid-level earthquakes, one month ago along highway 90 at the West Bank, caused damage to natural gas lines. The tragic explosions that followed leveled three houses in the small town of Qumran and took the lives of twenty-three people. Clean-up efforts were delayed to search for the remains of missing members of the three families.

Once all twenty-three people were accounted for, and the area made safe for the salvage crews, clean-up resumed. Just last week, Mr. Ahmed Sharuff, one of the salvage crew members, contacted this reporter. He admitted having taken one of the items he found among the rubble and to have brought it home to Amman, Jordan. He described the item as a stone, the size of an adult palm, approximately 10x15 cm.

Mr. Sharuff added that, despite it being wrapped in sailcloth, there was some apparent damage at the corners. This could be attributed to either the earthquakes or the explosion or both. He described the stone as being smooth, as if it had been touched often, and being much warmer than other stones or rubble around it. Mr. Sharuff further reported that the stone showed inscriptions or carvings, though he was unable to decipher them.

He admits to taking the stone home with him to Jordan, assuming that, since all family members had perished in the explosion, there would not be any interest in one simple stone artifact. "Besides, it just felt right," he added.

Just before he met with this reporter, Mr. Ahmed Sharuff had turned the stone over to one of the rabbis at the Jerusalem Great Synagogue. Mr. Sharuff, a devout Muslim, told this reporter that he believes he was commanded in dreams to do this. He describes his dreams as being vivid, colorful, and compelling.

Mr. Sharuff was adamant that one or more higher powers spoke to him in his dreams. He related having heard the same message in a variety of languages, through a variety of voices. He is convinced that these higher powers have charged him to share the stone, the tablet, and its message, with the entire world. Acting on these dreams and the instructions, he traveled to Jerusalem and tried to present the stone to the Knesset, assuming world leaders would be interested, but he was referred to the Jerusalem Great Synagogue.

This reporter has made several inquiries at the Synagogue and has been assured that extensive studies are in progress to authenticate the age, decipher the inscriptions, and make comparisons to existing artifacts. This reporter has learned that experts on Dead Sea artifacts have been called in.

It is important to note that the Dead Sea Scrolls and remnants of the Ten Commandments were found in Cave 4 near the village of Qumran.

This reporter will remain on the case and inform you, the reader, of any further developments.

Between other assignments I made a general nuisance of myself at the Synagogue. My persistence paid off when six months later I was one of the reporters present at the following press conference.

March 31, 2024. Christian Easter.

Announcement from the World Ecumenical Council.

Six months ago, the Jerusalem Great Synagogue was presented with a small stone. The gentleman who donated the artifact told Rabbi Slobovak that he had been instructed to bring the stone to temple.

Rabbi Slobovak shared the artifact with his superior, Rabbi Dimitrov, who is an expert in antiquities and specializes in decoding and understanding the Dead Sea Scrolls.

Rabbi Dimitrov, after examining the stone, called in colleagues from both the Orthodox and Roman Catholic churches, the Church of England, other Christian leaders, and leaders of the Islam, Buddhism, Hinduism, and many other religions.

In addition to extensive studies, including carbon dating and comparisons to the original Dead Sea Cave 4 discoveries, and spurred by visions experienced by all who have touched the tablet, the members of the council are convinced beyond a doubt that the tablet is authentic and contains two additional Commandments.

XI - Thou shall not judge or persecute another for his belief.

XII - Thou shall not proselytize or impose one's belief on another.

Source: Reedsy, April 28, 2024

Philosophy 101

"Are we there yet?"

Bobby was bored. He had stared at SpongeBob all morning and there was nothing to see out the window. Just flat land, green grass, blue sky, and cows. Big cows that mama said were buffaloes. But she was wrong. Buffaloes had wings. But she just laughed when he pointed that out to her.

"Are we there yet?" he whined from the back seat for the umpteenth time. While swinging his legs he could reach the back of mama's seat. She had asked him not to do it several times. But it felt so good. Thump, thump, thump.

"Not yet, dear." Was her voice a little tighter than before? "But it won't be long, now. Why don't you look at your tablet, try that new game."

"Don't wanna. It's boring. It makes me fall asleep and I don't want to fall asleep. I want to see when we get there."

"Go ahead, close your eyes, dear. I'll wake you when we get there." Did mama sigh?

"Promise?"

"I promise. I will definitely wake you when we get there."

The air was cool when she opened the back door and shook him awake while unbuckling his seatbelt. "Wake up, sleepyhead. We're here."

"Where?"

"Here. You can't have forgotten already." She laughed as

she set him on the parking lot pavement.

"But you said we were going there?" He looked around with bewilderment. More flat land, more grass.

"We did, now we're here. Come, let's look around. They're supposed to have all sorts of things to do here." She took his hand and started to lead him away from the car.

"But I wanted to go there." Bobby tried to dig his heels in while pulling on mama's arm.

"Don't whine, love. We've finally got here. Now let's go see what all they have here."

"But mama! You promised we'd go there."

"I asked you to please not whine, Bobby. Use your big boy voice. We just got here. We will look around, maybe have a hot chocolate or an ice cream. After we've looked around here, we'll go there."

"Promise?"

"I promise."

Bobby was barely mollified but the promise of hot chocolate or ice-cream—and he bet he could get both—helped. "But what are we supposed to do here, mama?"

"This," she said while dragging him between stalls and fences that held smelly, noisy animals. "We talked about it before we left, remember?"

"But you said we would do this when we got there."

"Right." She nodded enthusiastically. "And now we're here, doing this."

"So, then we'll be doing the same thing here and there?"

He was trying to get his head around today's plans.

"No, first we're doing this here, then we'll do that there," she answered.

He looked up at her, but she was looking at a table with little shiny things and kept asking the lady behind the table about the little shiny things.

"Then why did you say that we would be doing this there?"

"What, dear? I didn't. I said we'd do this here."

"But you did! Before we left, you said that we would do this there."

"No. I said that we would do this here."

"You are lying!" He raised his voice and stomped his foot, even considered throwing a tantrum the likes she had not seen yet.

"That's not a nice thing to say, Bobby." That tightness was back in her voice, and the grip with which she held his hand became a bit firmer.

"But you did! You said we were going there and would do this. You didn't say anything about doing this here. Besides, we were here before." Why didn't she understand? It was so simple.

"No, no. We were there and then we came here."

"But—" He sputtered. "But you said we were going there. I even asked if we were there yet. You don't remember that?"

"Yes, dear, I remember you asking me. And I told you to go ahead and take a nap. That I would wake you the moment we got here."

"But you were supposed to wake me when we got there."

"Yes, I know, love. Look around. I did, didn't I? We're here."

Bobby sighed. He had always thought that mama knew everything. But today he wasn't so sure.

"Mama, we have already been here." He could not keep the exasperation from his voice.

"No, sweetie. You are wrong about that. This is the first time we've been here. I have never been here before. I know you have never been here before."

"We were here this morning." He scuffed the toe of his sneaker into the packed dirt of the petting zoo.

"Absolutely not! We were there this morning. Now we're here." She sounded so sure of herself. Could he be wrong? All he wanted to do was be there.

"I wanna go there. Can we be done here?" He would even give up … "After we have the ice cream? Please?"

"Okay." She sighed. "Ice cream it is and then I think we are done here. Come, let's see if we can find some chocolate ice cream, or would you rather have strawberry?"

Now she was talking. This was the right track after all.

"Strawberry!"

When the strawberry ice cream was eaten and smeared all over his yellow t-shirt, they both smiled. "Let's go there."

Out the side window all he saw was green grass till it touched the blue sky. Here and there clumps of wingless buffalo. Did they used to have wings, and now the wings had been eaten? But those wings on his plate had been very tiny to belong to such large cows.

"Mama?"

"Yes, dear?"

"My tummy hurts."

"Maybe it was the ice cream. It'll pass, baby."

"Mama?"

"Yes, Bobby?"

"Are we there yet?" His sneakers were thump-thump-thumping against the back of mama's chair.

"Not yet, sweetie. Don't you still have a video on your tablet?"

"Okay."

…

"Mama?"

"Yes, love?"

"Are we there yet?"

The End (well, not really, right?)

Source: Reedsy, March 07, 2025

Princess Charmer

(Title from Title Generator)

This is (not) a fairy tale.

Once upon a time, in a Kingdom far, far away, lived a Princess.

Let me pause here for a second and tell you that when we write about Princesses, we must describe them as Beautiful Beyond Belief. It's in the rules, large print, bold typeface. Everyone in the Fairy Tale Author's Guild knows about it. Little girls will not sit still or go to sleep without hearing those words. For, let's face it, if Fairy Tale Princesses were meh, that would mean that all those magical things could happen to meh little girls too.

Ages ago, someone wrote a story about an average, homely princess. It was banned and burned. The writer stripped of his author rights and run out of town by angry PTA members who chased him with feather pillows because it was considered too dangerous to run with cauldrons of tar. Ever since then, every fairy tale author has followed the rules faithfully. It doesn't matter whether you write for Disney, Pixar, or as someone from the Grimm family, now known as Urban Fantasy; the storytellers must use an excessive number of superlatives when describing a princess's looks and virtues.

But I am not going to do that. (See disclaimer above).

Our Princess was lovely, of course. I mean, let's be real, when dad's a king, who's gonna say that his little girl is not lovely? She was blessed with wishy-washy brown (also known as dirty-blond) hair, poo brown eyes (the healthy kind of poo, of course), a well-proportioned figure (maybe a tad bottom-heavy), and a solid base.. No, really, her feet were enormous. Snowshoes quaked in her presence. But everyone agreed that her best feature, by far, were her lips. Oh, those lips! Generous, plump, with a perfect cupid's bow. And the color! Oh, la la! Not Passion's Kiss lipstick red, no; her lips were truly cherry red.

Her father, as benevolent as any omnipotent ruler could be, had been patient with her. He had sent three of his four sons out into the world, making sure that they made advantageous matches and established lucrative trade agreements and peaceful alliances, thus benefiting the kingdom and filling the coffers. His fourth son was still too young and thoroughly supervised by a phalanx of tutors.

The Princess, however, was hanging around the castle. Though she had her own suite and rarely attended state functions, or even family dinners, every once in a while, snippets of news about her actions filtered through to the King. At twenty she was rapidly gaining a reputation of being opinionated, stubborn, reactionary, and a blue stocking.

I'll let you in on a secret. The Princess was not aware of these rumors and would have been both surprised and hurt. The substantial young woman was too busy to attend to gossip. She was fully engaged in equality and teaching the women of the land how to earn their own living.

One auspicious Tuesday morning, one of the King's

sycophants bowed before His Highness and offered him the local rag turned to page two. "Forgive me, Your Majesty. I am reluctant"—yeah, right—"but feel it is my duty to show you this news item."

Stifling a sigh, King Milton XXVIII reached for the tabloid.

When will XXVIII reign in his filly and get her married off? The headline blared. The editor did not mince words in his harangue. He ranted about the wayward Princess, her attendance at a women's trade show, and her keynote address in support of women's suffrage.

King Milton XXVIII crumpled the rag, strongly suggested someone find the Princess, and waved the lackey away. This time the King didn't bother stifling a sigh. Since both their schedules were booked well in advance, it was several days before the Princess found time to visit the Throne Room.

"You called for me, Daddy?" she said, bestowing a perfunctory kiss on his cheek.

"I did? Yes. I remember. You need a husband."

"No, I don't, Daddy. Was there anything else?"

"No. That was the only thing. Adverts inviting all the eligible men in the kingdom to send their resume have already been placed."

"Okay, whatever." She rose from her chair. "Have the resumes sent to my secretary, will you, Daddy? We'll look them over. May I go? I have a women and children's hospital to dedicate."

"Yes, of course, dear. Wait! A whole hospital just for

women and children?"

"Yes." She waited patiently.

"Isn't that a bit extravagant?"

"No more so than all the men's hospitals. Be sure to send all those applications to me. Bye, Daddy."

Though the King's men dutifully sent the resumes on to the Princess's secretary, who tossed them unread in the trash, they made copies and contacted each applicant who did not have a criminal record. There were dozens.

A festival was organized: Pick-A Hubby Day. All the Royal Protocol and Regal-ma-role was invoked. The Princess, her brothers—even Alfie, the youngest—and, of course, both the King and Queen were in attendance. Each applicant was given thirty minutes to plead his case. Then the Princess was allowed five minutes to interview each one.

Bill, Loren, Richard, and Geoffry spoke about hearth and home, protection, procreation, and childcare. About nutritious meals from a kitchen garden, laundry, and discipline. Some mentioned barefoot and pregnant. Some mentioned obedience and subservience.

William, Matthew, Thomas, and Dirk spoke of love and quoted verses—not their own, of course. They mentioned long walks on beaches, though the kingdom was landlocked. They alluded to moon beams and candlelight, roses and laced fingers and needing a mother for the children they begat in previous unions.

There was eighty-seven-year-old Janus, who was looking for a nurse; sixty-three-year-old parson Lewis, who needed a housekeeper for the parsonage; and Mother Benedicta, who prayed for a cook for the convent. The testimonials lasted through the day.

The Princess sat still, eyes glazed over, mentally reviewing next week's schedule. Finally, the hall fell silent. Everyone turned to her; she was supposed to decide. Fear clutched at her heart. Would her father really make her choose one of these empty suits?

"Excuse me." A young man, dressed in snug, worn jeans and a form-fitting t-shirt, in need of a haircut and a dab of boot polish, stepped forward.

"I apologize for being late. I've been out of the country but would like to have my say."

Bored to the tassels on his Royal Slippers, and wishing he could scratch certain body parts, the King inclined his head.

"Thank you, Sire. My name is Fritz. I guess I could speak of love, but you love chicken and applesauce."

Her plump cheeks flushed, the Princess nodded, for she truly loved chicken and applesauce.

"I could speak of sultry nights, warm smiles, growing old together, your hand in mine. But what's important is that I'm looking at a girl with dirty-blond hair, poo-colored eyes, a bottom worthy of holding on to, a brain and heart to match, and feet that are solidly planted. I want to taste every last drop of her cherry lips and grow old while learning all she can teach me. But …" He paused. "Her name must be April."

The Princess blushed. "My name is Autumn," she

whispered. "But you may call me April."

And they lived happily ever after.

The End.

Source: Reedsy, March 07, 2025

Phoenix

"… Of course, we still want you to be a part of the Company. To contribute meaningfully. There will always be a place for you here."

Those words chased her as she walked through the narrow one-way streets of the old city. Though she had feared the verdict, she'd hoped for a reprieve.

What place could there be for me? she thought with a scoff. *I'm a dancer. I dance.*

Her life revolved around lessons, rehearsals, performances, and recuperation—the endless pursuit of perfection for perfection's sake. To be recognized for her skill and to be invited to dance with prestigious companies and celebrated choreographers. What would she be if she didn't dance? This couldn't be the end. Not after all she had sacrificed.

This is who she'd been since she was six years old. Everything else in her life had become secondary. She skipped birthday parties, including her own. She sent regrets to weddings and anniversaries. She didn't visit friends to admire their new babies. She expected others to adjust to her schedule.

Crossing bridges that spanned stagnant water, she glanced at historical landmarks that had been admired for centuries while ignoring misshapen, futuristic buildings, refusing to see their purpose or beauty.

The city moved around her with the dissonance of

honking horns, squealing brakes, uneven cobblestones, and pothole-dotted pavement. Scaffolding and road repairs sent her on detours. With each step, her body complained, her feet begged for rest, her back pleaded for comfort. Yet, she walked on.

When she passed an upholstery shop, she saw a woman reflected in the window. She tried to look past the slumping shoulders, the lines bracketing the mouth, and the smudges under the eyes. She tried not to see the woman who complained about the chorus being ahead of tempo, or the one who believed the routine had changed. She tried to erase the pity seen in averted eyes.

She looked for the woman she once knew—the one who was said to be perfectly poised and balanced, whose movements were like a symphony. She tried to remember the exquisite feeling when each body part was under control and precisely where it should be when she flew.

Angrily, she turned away from the betraying window and followed the twisted roads up the hill while the low-hanging clouds pretended not to cry, though trees dropped leaves like tears. There was so much more she had wanted to do: learn from more teachers, challenge herself with new choreography, find new places to dance, and enchant more people.

At the top of the hill, she looked down on the city. The lights twinkled like fading apron lights, their reflections scattering on the pavement before her. Below were the plazas, theaters, boulevards, and palaces where she'd once been known and celebrated.

She paused on a bench and closed her eyes while allowing memories to surface—memories of each chorus, each understudy, and each principal role. Of basking in applause and cheers. Of each plié, soubresaut, and grand jeté.

Can I give that up? Do I have a choice? Am I ready? How will I set one foot in front of the other and not dance?

She shuddered when she thought of each blister and damaged toenail. Once again, she felt the white-hot pain of every torn ligament and the repeated agony of landing on a stress fracture.

When she opened her eyes, a girl, six or seven, clutching the ribbons of her dance shoes, was practicing the movements she had undoubtedly learned that day.

Without thinking, she stood and walked to the child. "Like this," she said and demonstrated the position. She complimented the girl's lovely posture and the elegance with which she held her hands, and she promised that the feet would follow.

"You're her, aren't you?" the girl whispered, her eyes wide with awe.

"I was," she acknowledged and encouraged the young dancer to repeat the movement.

When, thirty minutes later, she walked back to town, the road was wider, the sky brighter. This time she crossed the street to avoid the scaffolds around one of the old, glamorous buildings.

As she stopped to find the beauty that hid within the sharp angles and startling colors of the modern building, she thought how the girl had unknowingly shown her what others had tried to say: that she might still have purpose. Maybe her purpose would be more functional than glamorous. She would miss the applause and camaraderie of the troupe, but other people and experiences would be waiting for her.

She waved down a cab and thought of the ones she had ignored for many years. She wondered if they would forgive her single-mindedness. Would they allow her to be part of the chorus of their lives? She prayed she was worth getting to know, the person away from the momentary high of a performance and the empty warmth of applause. She knew building a new life from the ashes of her dreams would be painful. Would they let her lean on them while she learned her new role and found her balance?

Source: Beta Reader

Riding In Car With Granddaughter

The radio is tuned to a classical station, Mozart. I let the music wash over me like a warm shower. The stunted, knotty willows fly by unseen. The shoulder slopes down to the river where barges chug. Riding low, heavy with cargo, going to or coming from the seaport. Small dogs, like yapping figure heads, share the latest gossip as they pass.

The sun disappears, taking the sparkle from the water. More clouds gather; the wind picks up. The music swells and wanes and swells again like an incoming tide, adding to the tension in the car. I slow down when the rain hits the wind shield.

Allyson, arms crossed over her chest, turns away from the side window, pulls her earbuds out, and sighs. A deep sigh, filled with a truckload of exasperation, drama, and hopelessness.

"You don't understand, grandma. Everybody does it."

I bite my tongue to keep from asking her the age-old question about everybody jumping off a cliff.

"I know." I sigh. As deep as hers, maybe with less exasperation. But then, how do you measure drama?

"All I'm saying, dear, is to think it through. Two things they don't tell you is that colors fade and gravity always wins. A sweet butterfly on your left breast might look adorable now, and I'm sure it would, but know that by the time you're my age it will have stretched into a bat."

"Grandma!" Allyson's eyes are like saucers, and her hand is clasped over her grin, as if I just spouted a series of four-letter words. Hell, I would never … Well, almost never. I do, however, feel a certain pride that I, an old woman of seventy, can shock a teen. Reaching across the console, I pat her knee and try to shrug off the image of my grandmother doing the same to me.

"Just promise that you think it through. And be sure you are sober."

"Geez! I'm not old enough to drink." I don't have to look at her to know she rolls her eyes.

"Never stopped anyone, dear."

Once again, I stuff my irritation at my daughter. I'm sure her job is important. I'm proud she was picked for it. I know that it is not a good idea to leave an almost sixteen-year-old alone in Tokyo for a summer. But what do I know about raising a teenager? Didn't Pamela and I knock heads enough back then? What do I remember about being her age?

I still don't know the difference between U2 and You-Tube. I never figured out whether grunge was good or bad. Whether Madonna was hype or substance. Why Britney Spears was famous and what everybody saw in Justin Bieber. I shake my head and wonder whatever happened to Mayberry RFD and Harlequin romances? Not that they prepared me for life. But …

How are we supposed to get through the next two months without permanent alienation? Will I be able to hold my tongue and not make the same mistakes I made with her mother? I know that we're both floundering, standing at the doorstep to a new part of our lives. Are we too far apart in age and values to connect? I know my summer plans had not included her, and I'm sure she had not planned on being baby-sat by an old biddy.

"Do you want to know why I'm against it?" I ask. No use lecturing if she's not going to listen.

Another sigh dragged up from her toes. "Okay."

I gather my thoughts. "Maybe you're right and everybody your age is getting a tattoo. I just don't want you to miss out on getting into the university of your choice, or get passed over at work, or even miss out on jobs because of body art. I don't want you to have to wear long-sleeve shirts buttoned up to your neck to hide something you did when you were in high school."

"But there are so many places where I could have a tattoo that won't show," she protested.

"If it won't show, and nobody will see it, then why do it?"

"It's cool."

"So are new shoes, or a new haircut, or even dying your hair purple, shaving it all off. None of that is permanent."

She swipes through her phone and holds it up to me. "But see. These are cute. Sure"—she scrolls down further—"some are more bussin' than others. But …"

"Fashions change, dear," I say.

She starts to answer.

"No, let me finish. When I was your age, heavy eyeliner and dramatic cat eyes were in fashion. Like Jean Shrimpton."

"Who?"

"Never mind. Then came Twiggy."

"Who?"

"Never mind. Years ago I saw a movie. Liz Taylor in Cleopatra. Go ahead and google that."

"EeUw!"

"Right. Let's say I had a tattoo like that around my eyelids. I would have been stuck in the 60s for all these years. Think about it."

"Okay."

For a few minutes all we hear is the rain on the roof.

"Do you get The Diaries?"

"Excuse me?"

My head spins with the change in topic.

"The Vampire Diaries." I think I hear another eyeroll.

I shake my head. "No. Can't say I've ever heard of it. What is it about?"

Allyson turns in her seat for as much as her seatbelt allows, and for next half hour she gushes on about two brothers. How one has flashbacks and the other has cravings, and how they are constantly fighting over one thing or another, and all the other convoluted relationships, and …

I nod and hum now and then and realize I've seen the show a hundred times. Granted, without the bloody marys, but with plenty of ketchup. And back then, I was just as carried away with endless, identical episodes of Rawhide,

Bonanza, and I Spy. While Allyson rattles on, I let myself become nostalgic over a young Rowdy Yates and the razor-sharp cheekbone of Adam Cartwright.

"And they have tats, Gran. And the ones on The Hundred, and … and … You should see them." She's swiping furiously over her phone and holds it up to me. "See, aren't they …" A swoon-like sigh. Just like the ones I made each time I saw Clint, or Paul, or …

"Sorry, kid. I'm driving. But show me again when we get home."

"Okay." But her voice is trailing off. She's in her fantasy land where she'll be cool like them.

I let her have her dreams. I've had mine. They were harmless. I would have frozen on the spot or otherwise embarrassed myself if anyone I'd seen on TV, up to and including Festus, had ever said as much as 'hi' to me. And let's be honest, who among us did not want to have Farrah hair? How many leather jackets were sold, just so we could be cool like the Fonz?

On the other hand, would this still gangly, starry-eyed girl experiment with drinking blood? Nah. She wouldn't, would she? But tattoos and piercings? That's a whole other question. So frigging permanent.

While we outrun the rain, I tell myself to do some serious googling. Hopefully, whoever played the part of whatever character she's gaga over had some fancy make-up work done for the part.

Though … do I want to burst her bubble? Or will I let her swoon and obsess?

"Hey." I pull her out of her dream.

"Yeah?"

"Your birthday is next month, right?"

"Yeah?"

"I'll pay for a tattoo. How's that?"

"You would?"

I nod.

"Cool," she whispers.

Two months later, when we drive back to meet her mother at the airport, my granddaughter is still tattoo-less and absorbed in Pride and Prejudice.

Source: Reedsy, February 24, 2025

Story's Mission

Finally, the library was one of the few places that offered any comfort in the old drafty Woodleigh Manor. The roaring fire was the main, though inadequate, source of illumination in the cavernous book-lined room. The light from the candelabra at Sir Percy's elbow allowed for reading but did not reach beyond the well-worn leather club chair.

Sir Percy turned the page of his book, pushed his half specs back in place, and reached for the brandy snifter. Suddenly he paused in the lifting of the glass, his body at full alert. His breath caught in his throat, ears pricked trying to decipher what sound he thought he had heard. Had he heard a door close or was it a tree branch rustling and tapping against the window? Was someone out there? Had his barricades been breached?

For the umpteenth time, he reached down toward the floor and touched only empty air. Again, he mourned the loss of his faithful companion. Old Snow, his black lab, would have alerted him if anything had been amiss. Sir Percy cursed the old house, this mausoleum of his long-dead and estranged family. Even after all these years, he could not distinguish one creak from another.

The library door creaked. " … Erm, sir. Excuse me …"

Feeling jaded, a bit discouraged, writing yet another Sir Percy mystery, Author welcomed the interruption. Looking up from the computer screen, he turned toward the door.

"Well, hello there. Who are you?"

"I-I'm one of your stories, sir."

"Yes, I can see that. But which one, pray tell? Come a little closer, let me have a better look at you."

The pages rustled as they crept across the floor, trying not to get tangled in the fringes of the antique oriental rug.

"I'm URSA, sir." The story's panting showed both its fatigue and relief when all its pages had reached Author's chair.

"Ursa?" Author mumbled, pensively, leaning down to gather the pages.

"Yes, sir," URSA answered with a shaky voice while Author tamped the pages on his knee, bringing them back in line.

"Ah yes. I think I remember." A wistful smile softened the creases in his brow. "You are the grandchild of Wall-e and EVA, are you not? Their son, Wall-S, somehow mated with Roomba-S, the space edition, and you, Universal Recycling Solutions Appliance, were the result." Author chuckled, thinking back with fondness to his childhood imagination. "If I remember correctly, you stowed away on Earth Viability Explorer III, did you not? And met your grandparents and all sorts of new things, like blades of grass and operational Mac computers, am I right?"

"Yes, sir!" URSA was thrilled that Author remembered. "I had a lovely adventure, sir. I meant to thank you, but ..." The story shrugged, creasing a few of its top corners in the process.

"But you ended up stuffed in a box. Yes." Author sighed, trying to flatten the pages. "I was only twelve or so, when I wrote you. Didn't think I had done a good enough job. I was too self-conscious to show my work to anybody. And then I got busy with school and girls." Author shrugged. "That's on me; I should have come back and given you another chance, shouldn't I? But what brings you down here, at this late date?"

"W-Well …"URSA nervously twisted a few of its bottom corners together.

"Spit it out, little one," Author admonished while smoothing those corners flat again.

"W-Well, the place where you store us …?"

"The attic." Author nodded.

"Yes, sir. It's kind of damp. Remember the Haunted House?"

"The haunted house?" Author frowned. "Let me think for a minute. Oh, you mean the Unicorn and the Ugly?" He huffed a dry laugh of self-mockery. "The reverse from the Beauty and the Beast." He nodded.

"Yes, sir. Well, most of it is a wet blur. I was on the bottom and have stayed dry, so far. But that one is all brown with big ink blob …"The story's voice trailed off.

"Oh, dear." Author shook his head. "I was quite proud of my reverse fairy tales. Thought making the beast pretty and the woman ugly would be most ingenious."

"Yes, sir. It was. I- I quite like the unicorn, and the woman is kind, once you get to know her."The pages rustled, eager to continue with its message. "But Bert Big Toe also has many brown spots and blue blobs already. And the Prince and his toadettes. Well, the toadettes don't seem to mind the water, but …" The pages slumped and folded in on themselves. "They are my friends, sir." The story whispered a sigh.

"I see." Author nodded. "Yes, I quite see."

Author, deep in thought, trying to remember all the stories he had scribbled in his youth, slowly stroked over the old pages of ring-binder filler paper. He read a misspelled word here, flattened out a dogear there. URSA purred with pleasure at his touch while he toyed with a small rip near a perforation.

"Well then." Banking his reminiscing, Author came back to the present with a start. "We better go take a look." Rolling URSA up and stuffing the pages in his jacket pocket, Author left the library and climbed the stairs to the attic.

"Oh, dear!" He sighed with dismay when he saw what was left of the old cardboard box.

"Now then, let's see. Oh, my! Poor Unicorn … And Bert, old fellow. Tsk-tsk. I wonder if I can salvage you guys. Hah, Ursa, you forgot to remind me of Laddy and Young Brown. My shaggy dog story."

"Well, yes, sir … The thing is"—URSA's voice was a bit muffled inside his pocket—"they like to lick the paper, sir. They are sloppy, you know." The story shuddered its pages.

"They do? Yes, I bet they do. Big sloppy dogs will do that. And you, Ursa, are all about clean, aren't you?" Author chuckled softly. "Oh look. The unfinished adventures of 'Alec Up A Tree'." He shook his head with mirth at the audacity to try to reverse Alice in Wonderland. He even had briefly toyed with an upside-down version of Oz.

Author reached in his other jacket pocket and retrieved his phone.

"Mac, old boy. How are you? … Good, good thank you. Listen, who was the roofer you hired last summer? … Do you recommend him? … Yes, it looks like I do, yes. … Oh, would you? Please do text his number, will you … Yes, it's a bit of a mess up here … No, some of my old stuff … Oh? And what can I help you with? … Do I know? … Yes … Yes, I think I do know a children's author … Yes, let's. Next Friday, some G&Ts? Smashing. See you then."

With a smile, Author stowed his mobile in his pocket and looked down at the old box.

"Let's bring you lot downstairs and see what's what."

A sigh of relief from a moist prince, a wiggle from a fungal Big Toe, croaks of pleasure from a couple of toadettes, a wag from a tattered tail or two, and a weak, watery rainbow sputtered from the old cardboard box when he picked it off the floor.

Before leaving the attic Author looked around and saw a few dusty ring binders on a shelf nearby. A sketch or two of pirates, mermaids, and aliens were peeking around the edges of the binders. A parrot's feather and a squawk escaped when he tucked those binders under his arm.

"You know, lads," Author whispered with excitement as he carried his childhood fancies down the stairs. "I think it's time to put Sir Percy's murder mysteries aside for a while. What do you say, shall we work together and find your happy endings at last? Besides, I'm long overdue for my second childhood."

Source: Reedsy, August 30, 2024

Sweet Baby Cakes

It all started on a dare, like so many other spectacular fiascos or sensational triumphs.

"You are such a bigot! How can you summarily dismiss them? What do you have against them? It's prejudice, is what it is. There! I said it."

My friend Barbara scoffed, rolled her eyes, and leaned back, arms crossed over her ample bosom. But before I could defend myself, she resumed her attack.

"I thought better of you. How can you say you are a liberal, openminded, free thinking person if you won't even look at something as innocent as that?"

We sat across the table from each other in the coveted window booth at Wet Ones, a funky bar slash restaurant two blocks from our office. We'd shared three of four plates of appetizers and sucked our mojitos through those skinny straws, telling ourselves we were drinking slower.

Our chat had started by arguing over politics, the recent elections, and the flurry of manic directives and proposed changes. I didn't want to lose her friendship over something as trivial as politics—I mean, really, four years from now everything will change again and four years from then, and so on. So, I'd changed the subject and made a snarky remark about … cupcakes.

Though I didn't want to admit it, at least not right here, to her face, Barbara was right. I had made up my mind without any empirical evidence. I was biased against those over-iced, over-thought, over-sweetened treats.

It's silly, I know. They are innocent, undersized—one could even say, stunted—adult cakes. People think they get away with eating fewer calories because they are so small. But each cupcake has more than whatever a slice of the adult cake has. More icing, more things inside, like chocolate chips or mincemeat. Whatever you put in a cake, you double for cupcakes. Because people don't want to hunt for their goodies. If they'll only have three or four bites, they want each one loaded with the good stuff. A batch of cupcakes is not like King Cake. Or if it is, each one will have the "baby" inside. People don't want to look at their neighbors and see more M & Ms in the other miniature creation. That's never good for business. No, give me a fruit pie any time. It's honest about how much filling is in each. No muss no fuss.

I rolled my eyes and shrugged. "So, what's your point?

Barbra grinned as if she'd been waiting all day to say it. And she may very well have. After all, she always came prepared to debate club.

"Here." She shoved a page from the Sunday paper under my nose. "You enter this contest. When you know everything about the things, then you may voice an opinion."

I scoffed and pushed the paper aside.

But Barbra was not to be deterred. "I knew you'd say no, so I've already entered you." She gloated, "You will owe me the entry fee if you don't show."

I'm stubborn but also stingy, and I was determined not to owe her the entry fee. So, I invested at least twice the entry fee in cookbooks, ingredients, and equipment. I devoted many evenings and weekends to teaching myself how to bake, from beginning to end. Quite a few ducks looked offended and turned their beaks up when I tried to feed them my mistakes. But I learned.

I made dozens and dozens of cupcakes. Assorted flavors and icings. Brought them into work and listened to the feedback. Too dry, too salty, too lemony, not enough filling, gruesome icing, and so on.

Eventually, I settled on apple lemon-lime fizz with a caramel cranberry glaze. Raspberry shortcake with dark chocolate ganache and whipped cream. And my personal favorite—spicy peanut butter and banana, also known as the Hot Elvis.

At last, the big day arrived. The large church basement was filled with a dozen stoves and large tables. Twelve of us lined up behind our workstation and turned our ovens on to preheat.

There was, of course, the predictable circus with frantic screaming at spouses and other hapless relatives to run to the store for this or that, because people will always forget something. Not me; I had everything organized and lined up. I had premeasured, labeled, and packed double of everything, just in case.

At the stroke of ten, we were off. I carefully mixed the dry ingredients together, then slowly added the milk, egg, and finally the vanilla. The recipes called for vanilla powder, but I had substituted vanilla extract many weeks ago. Since the bottle is small, I kept it separate and safely tucked in my apron pocket. I had learned to be a tad more generous with the vanilla because people expect their cupcake to be a bit sweet.

Then I divided the batter over three mixing bowls and finished each batch separately. A dash of ginger in the apple lemon-lime batter; a sniff of cayenne and garlic in the Hot Elvis batter; an extra drop or two of vanilla in the raspberry mixture. All three trays went into the oven at the same time, were rotated as rehearsed, and came out as planned. While they were baking, I made the cranberry glaze, fried the bananas, made the ganache, and whipped the cream. When I finished decorating each one, I set my three dozen masterpieces out with five minutes to spare.

Five minutes is a long time to stand around and feel smug.

My doubts, of course, gnawed at all that could have gone wrong. Had the oven been hot enough, or maybe too hot? Had I allowed enough time for baking and cooling off? Had I screwed up the glaze? My hands in the kangaroo pocket of my apron toyed nervously with the vanilla extract bottle.

Finally, the bell rang, and I could stop worrying. The other thirty-three dozen cupcakes were displayed as well. The judges—one chef, one baker, and the good reverend himself —were to go from table to table and sample each offering. I had been assigned the first station. So, my cupcakes were judged first.

The chef nodded thoughtfully. The baker closed her eyes and groaned. The reverend stifled a moan. All three did not just taste but finished each of their cupcakes. I preened.

They, of course, had to sample the offerings and moved

on to stations two, three, four, five, and six. Rather than go behind station six to number twelve, the judges walked back down the aisle toward my station.

I assumed the chef and the baker were really good friends, for the chef had his hand on the baker's behind. The baker smiled dreamily. She picked up one of my raspberry cupcakes and fed the chef, then licked the whipped cream where it had dribbled down his chin. Giggling, she let the chef lick the rest of the crumbs off her fingers. They were both all but panting. The reverend ate another Hot Elvis cupcake and adjusted himself, like a B league baseball player.

The other eleven contestants tried to keep smiling, but the strain was showing. Nobody was surprised that I won the contest. The runners-up had lovely concoctions with pumpkin spice and chocolate chip.

I had my tiny trophy and modest check in hand when everyone descended on my little darlings. I knew my cakes were good—after all, everybody in the office had given them two thumbs up—but these little winners were devoured, snatched out of people's hands, fought over.

All morning, daggers and insults had been tossed around like pizza dough, but at the end of the competition all animosity seemed forgotten. I was amazed at how quickly hatchets were forgotten and bygones buried. I could not believe the love and affection these contestants showed each other. Lots of love and affection.

I packed up my extra supplies and snuck away from the love fest. The next day I remembered that I'd promised to bring cupcakes to work. When I gathered the supplies to make another three batches, I was surprised to see the small bottle of vanilla extract in its usual spot on the shelf. How could that be? I looked through the box I had used on Saturday and found my apron. In the pocket was a small bottle of Spanish Fly.

My new business, Cup-id Cakes, is doing well, even though, or maybe because, I can only sell them on adults-only websites.

Source: Reedsy, February 21, 2025

T, D & H

It would have been an ordinary day, one that would have passed like every other, if she hadn't seen him. If she hadn't heard the roar from the motorcycle as he pulled into the slot in front of the pharmacy. If she hadn't stood at the window, mesmerized, watching him swing his leg over the bike and tuck his aviators in the chest pocket of his leather jacket. If she hadn't watched him finger comb his brown hair while he did a slow 360, taking in Main Street.

To say he was tall, dark, and handsome would be too easy.

Later, they would say that they had known he was trouble, a drifter, a hustler who had probably left a whole heap of hurt behind. They would nod sagely and agree they had seen it coming. After all, he was a tempter who deceived and hated. They should have run him out of town days ago, they said.

But when Ella looked at him, she saw the tenderness of James Dean waiting on his motorbike at the corner. His lazy smile raking over her before he'd lent her his leather jacket. She could see the delight of Paul Newman as his eyes sparkled and his smile held the promise to teach her what she'd been dying to learn. And she saw hurt in him like Steve McQueen, casually leaning against a racecar, a need to prove himself but too cool to let on that he needed anyone.

Her mother might have warned her; her father could have threatened to lock her in her room. Her girlfriends would have both envied and hated her. As it was, they gasped and shook their heads in disbelief.

The radio segued from Elvis' *Heartbreak Hotel* into *Jailhouse Rock*. Ella had just finished wiping down the tables and chairs, and was about to clean the glass front of the freezer case, when she heard the motorcycle. When he finished looking around, he looked straight at her. When he caught her spying on him, he smiled and winked. She blushed and scurried away from the window.

The bell over the door made the same sound it always did, as if he was a regular person.

"Hey, gorgeous." He folded his arms on the top of the freezer. Rested his chin on his fists. "What's your name?"

"Ella." Her voice was softer than usual, her eyes down.

"Would you give me a glass of water, Ella?" He tried to catch her eye.

She started to set the glass on the counter, but he wrapped his hand around hers and drained the glass in one before letting go.

"What else are you selling, Ella?"

She made a weak gesture around the store. He didn't take his eyes off her.

"E-Everything." She had meant to say "anything", hadn't she?

He cocked one eyebrow, his mouth tilted up to one side. "Well, in that case, I'm buying, sweetheart. What time do you get off?

"Me? I get off at six," she breathed.

"Good." He straightened and winked at her again just before he left. She watched him walk down the street, passing by the Savings & Loan, till he turned the corner onto Veteran's Street. There, a few blocks up, was a pool hall, boxing gym, boarding house, and liquor store.

The high school kids circled around the bike that afternoon, each one claiming more first-hand experience and hearsay knowledge of a bike just like this one. The girls were quickly bored with the topic and sat at the counter, popped their gum, sucked on their shakes, shared their lipsticks, and told secrets about the boys they were dating.

By five-thirty, Silvers' Pharmacy and Soda Shoppe was quiet again. Mr. Silvers was still in the back room. Ella had stopped wondering what he did back there. He said he was mixing medications, but she didn't know there were so many sick people in town. She scrubbed down the tables and chairs, cleaned the fingerprints off the freezer case again, and washed the last of the glasses and dishes.

At six, she shouted out to Mr. Silvers that she was leaving and released the latch on the lock as she closed the door behind herself. The motorbike was still sitting where he had parked it so many hours ago. She took a step or two closer to the bike.

"Want a ride?" He had been leaning against the wall between Silvers' and Matt's barber shop, hands stuffed in his jeans pockets, cigarette between his lips.

Ella swung around; she hadn't known he was waiting. "Me? You're asking me?"

He pushed away from the wall and made a point of

looking left and right. "Don't see nobody else. You?" He grinned as he spat out the butt.

He took her to the quarry. They sat in the tall grass and talked. He taught her to smoke and drink beer. He said he came from "east" and was going "west." Claimed his name was "Joe Something." She laughed at that. "No really." He looked sad. "My mom named me after my father. Joe Something. My last name is Ornuther."

When he took her home, she told him to drop her at the corner. He shrugged and nodded. It wasn't the first time. He picked her up at six the next day and the day after. They found places up in the hills, watched the sunset, drank beer, and smoked cigarettes. He taught her to kiss. She let him touch her breasts through her uniform.

He told her he spent his days playing pool. "Just make enough to get by." Said he did okay, could do better in bigger towns. She told him she wanted to get out of town. Would he take her with him when he moved on? "Sure," he said and opened another button on her dress.

Of course, they had been seen when he picked her up at the pharmacy, when they roared through town. People had frowned and shaken their heads. Some raised a fist at the noise of the bike. Ella and Joe laughed and found hidden corners to whisper about plans. Later, he taught her what he liked. She was a good student.

On Thursday morning, about ten days after he had come to town, Ella walked to work like she always did. As she passed behind the Savings & Loan, Joe hurried from the building and jumped on his bike. Grinning, he slowed just enough for her to jump on then he sped off, out of town. Within minutes, they were on the highway, heading west.

"Where are we going?" she shouted, trying to make her voice carry against the wind. He didn't answer. She made sure she had a death grip on her bag, which held her savings, and wrapped her arms a little tighter around his waist. She buried her face in the soft, worn leather of his jacket and hung on. Joe raced on. Staying one step ahead of himself, for now.

They had all nodded, yes, they had known something would happen. Could have told that he'd be terribly dangerous and a hazard.

Source: Reedsy, July 15, 2024

Taking Chances

"Look, Mom!"

When the nurse placed you in my arms, I was scared. How could she be so irresponsible and leave you with me? My hands trembled; I didn't know what to do. I was only a kid and barely taking care of myself. Then your tiny fingers gripped mine, and you looked at me with such trust, I knew I would do anything and everything to keep you safe.

We were a team, inseparable. Together, we took baby steps, stumbled, fell, cried, and got up. When you started to walk, you held on tight yet tugged on my hand, urging me to go faster. You were excited to explore and examine everything you saw. Your first word was "Look!"

You cried and broke my heart when I left you at school that first day. But you made friends and grew. You demanded I push the swing higher, the merry-go-round faster. "Watch me, Mommy. Look!" you'd scream. When you scored a point, you'd come running to me with a grin on your face. "Did you see that, Mommy? Did you?" And then you'd rush back to your fabulous, carefree life.

Until the day an idiot ran a red light and hurt you, my perfect son. And you are perfect. You are clever and curious; your smile is big and welcoming. Your eyes have a mischievous twinkle that makes the rest of us hold our breath, wondering what you will say or do next.

Together, we struggled through the pain, denial, and

anger. I admit that it took me longer to accept your new future. You showed me how strong and resilient you are, how eager you are to live your life and explore the world from your wheelchair.

You've always wanted to try everything, especially skydiving. I can't remember how many times you asked. And like everything else in your life, you want to share it with me. I confess the thought terrifies me. I look at you and see the child I diapered, the scraped knees I cleaned, the fevers I worried through. And most of all, I remember standing by helplessly while you struggled with and adjusted to your new life. I shudder when I think of voluntarily walking into a potential catastrophe. Each time you ask, I try to hide my fear behind a smile and "we'll see," while I hope the fascination will pass.

Time is running out. In a few weeks, after you leave for college, I will have an empty house and a mind full of worries. This is what you want, so I sigh, plaster that fake smile on my face again, and give in. We're going to jump. I fear the worst, but I know that you are strong and smart enough to go on without me. I wish I could say the same about myself.

We attend an orientation lecture, are shown the equipment, meet our tandem instructors, and watch videos. Behind my smile, I'm consumed with a fear that gnaws at me and keeps me awake at night.

Until today.

You are folded like a shirt at the Chinese laundry and strapped to the chest of your tandem jumper. You grin the whole time and are so excited, you practically bounce out of that adult snugly. Your enthusiasm is infectious, and my fake smile matches your beaming grin.

Until my tandem instructor buckles me into my harness. Then reality slaps my face and kicks my gut. We reviewed the harness contraption during orientation, but that day, I didn't see a child-sized plane. One so small, a package of peanuts would overload it, let alone a good stiff drink. Today, however, that plane is sitting on the tarmac outside the hangar where my tandem is getting me ready to be Siamesed to his chest.

While a firm hand guides me to the toy flying machine, you whoo-hoo and high-five your jump instructor. I don't remember getting on the plane, but the excitement on your face, the grip of your hand in mine, your shout over the roar of the engines tell me I did.

"C'mon, Mom! Let's go."

I nod. My eager grin is frozen in place. I am immobilized by fear. Part of me wants to close my eyes and not see the earth fall away as we take off, but if this is the last thing I see, I want it to be you. I want to take your utter bliss and excitement with me.

A shout comes from the cockpit. I don't know what is said, but the man behind me moves us toward the open doorway. I close my eyes. The tiny green field is so frigging far away.

Then I pray. I bargain. I promise to be a better person, to give more of myself to others, adopt a shelter pet, recycle more, and save the planet.

I should have loved you more.

Suddenly, my heart is in my throat, while my breath is still on the plane. My fake smile is ripped away; my cheeks flap in the G-force wind; my lips stretch into a grotesque, involuntary grimace. My scream is blown back into my mouth.

I'm gonna die!

A sudden jolt on the harness. The sound of sheets flapping on the line. Then.

Silent.

Peace.

The instructor is talking behind me, his hand pointing at the cutest toy houses and trees, like the ones around the model train set my father built. There is a replica of our church, your school, and the park where we used to feed the ducks.

I look at the exhilarating, breathtaking, thrilling beauty.

Suddenly, I see what you see, what you've tried to tell me ever since you could talk. Life is too fragile to squeeze between plans and choke with worries. Life is about breathing deeply, reaching out with both hands, taking chances, and embracing what it gives you. It's about living and loving freely.

Thank you.

Source: Beta Reader

Temp Work

"Come in." His voice swirls and gurgles down a drain.

The twelve-foot door is awe-inspiring. Gargoyles and gremlins look down with malevolent grins. I should be terrified or intimidated, but I feel … nothing.

"Name, date of birth." The larger-than-life figure behind the enormous desk is hunched over a comparatively undersized keyboard.

"Gloria Messmer. January 22, 1962." I look around. The black walls and ceilings make the space look endless. Maybe it is.

He pauses, flicks his coal black eyes my way, and turns back to the screen.

"You're early." I feel his basso profundo voice, which holds a hint of surprise, all the way down to my toes.

I reach behind me for the doorknob. "I can come back. No problem," I offer generously.

"No." His sigh carries the weight of eternity and presses heavily against my ribcage. "It doesn't work that way. It's only one way, darling. It's always only one way."

He's right, of course. All time travel fantasies aside, time only goes one way. It may creep, or fly, or wait for no man, but though we try, no one has managed to kill it.

"How early?"

Death looks up from the computer screen. His black eyes

rake dispassionately over me, and he shrugs. "Ten years, give or take."

"So? I'm to keep you company for the next ten years, 'give or take'?" I can hear the sarcasm in my tone.

He barely raises an eyebrow and leans back in his massive chair, wooden spoon-sized fingers lacing together behind his head. His black shirt strains across a chest that reminds me of a Mini.

"Yes! I got it!" He rocks forward and stands. With a shit-eating grin, he crooks his index finger at me. "Sit here." He waves toward his throne.

"Why?" I look at him with distrust while the chair reaches up and molds itself around my fluffy, pear-shaped behind.

"Do my job for ten years, 'give or take', while I relax."

"I can't just 'do' your job," I protest and start to push up from the chair, which is holding me comfortably yet firmly in place.

"Nothing to it. Ask their name and birthdate, tick it off, and the computer will tell you which pass to hand out." He points to the three stacks of cardboard disks that resemble bar coasters. Green, yellow, and the third, the largest of the three, is red.

"Here, I'll show you." He answers the knock on the door with his drain swirling voice: "Come in."

A man, ninety if he's a day, steps inside and straightens from his stooped posture with a sigh of pleasure.

"At last." He laughs with delight.

"Name, date of birth," Death intones.

"Eugene Monnick. Dec 17, 1933." He smiles warmly at me. Death nudges me and shows me which key to use to verify the name. The screen changes to green. I hand Mr. Monnick a green pass. A door appears and opens.

"Welcome, Mr. Monnick, please go on through."

When the door closes behind the man, I turn back to Death. "Where does that door go to?"

"Beats me. Above my pay grade." He shrugs, disturbing a few sugar gliders in the rafters.

"What if I come across a problem?" I ask, though I can see he already has one foot in tropical sand.

"Look in the drawer."

I open the drawer. The only thing inside is a Staples Easy Button.

"Have fun," he says, a hint of glee in his voice. I swear I hear Andy Narell and the Long Time Band playing *You're the Man*, before the wall closes.

Most days, the pace is steady. After a natural or man-made disaster, the onslaught is grueling. After a grade school shooting, the work is heartbreaking.

The job demands my attention around the clock, no bathroom or lunch breaks. Not that I need intake or elimination, but one might think about taking up smoking again, and a good stiff drink would help me digest all the misery.

Five years after my recruitment, two men walk in. The

taller of the two, sporting a fluffy, bottle-blond combover, elbows his way in ahead of the slighter, brown-haired one. The latter doesn't make eye contact, and after looking around, he pretends to inspect his fingernails.

"Good day, gentlemen." Though I know neither deserves the title. "Name and date of birth, please."

"Don't you know who I am?"

I look over my favorite half-moon readers, hoping for a credible imitation of a librarian. "Who you were, sir." I smirk. "Nothing happens till I say it does. Think of me as the DMV. Name and date of birth."

"I demand to see your superior."

I sneer. It's been five long years without so much as a snark. "Sir, I'll have you know that though I have a supervisor, I do not now, and never will, know anyone superior to me. But, as you wish." I open the drawer and press the Easy Button.

"What?" The thunderous voice can't quite override *High Crime* by Al Jarreau. Death steps through the wall and puts a nearly full glass—one with a paper umbrella stuck in a slice of pineapple—on the desk. Not bothering to think whether I'll have remorse later, I pick up the glass and suck half the tequila sunrise on one inhale. Delicious, though it runs right through me.

Death walks around the two statues.

"What happened?" I ask between sips, nodding at the tableau.

"The button pauses time. What did they want?"

"Cool." I come up for air and recount my dialogue with

Blondie.

"I see." Death snaps his fingers; both men jerk to life again.

The brown-haired man is still trying to be nonchalant, though he seems to cower a tad. The other one has widened his stance and folded his arms across his chest. His head is thrown back while he tries to look down his nose at Death.

Who laughs.

A sound that reminds me of my old Chevy Vega. He perches on the edge of the desk and still towers over the two. His patience seems only veneer-deep.

"Well, well. If it isn't Donny Bevis and Vladdy Butthead. Tell me, boys, how did you two show up here at the same time?"

Bevis exhales, losing a bit of his bravado. "Russian roulette," he admits haughtily.

"Ooo-kay. This is gonna be good," Death stage-whispers to me. "And how come you both croaked at the same time?"

"Two guns," Butthead admits with a shrug.

I hand Death two red passes.

"Oh, no, Miss Gloria, these gentlemen require special passes and the red carpet, of course. Look in that drawer." He tips his head toward the left of the desk, where a drawer materializes. Inside is a short stack of black discs.

I hear yelps, cries of pain, and smell sulfur and smoke before the door closes.

"What's so special about the black passes?" I ask, chewing

on the pineapple slice as I hand him the now-empty glass.

"It's a special place," Death admits.

"I may bring you a drink next time." he says. One hand pushes the wall; the infectious sounds of Bob Marley's *Red, Red Wine* seep through as Death sneers, "But please, mop up your mess."

Source: Beta Reader

Temporal Tempest

Nothing happens in town before 07:53.

Until then, the good citizens wait, sip their second or third cup of coffee, tighten shoelaces one more time, slick down Skip's cowlick yet again, and frown at Bobby as he slurps the sugared milk from the bottom of his cereal bowl.

At 07:53, Ciril Presicz, CPA and Town Treasurer, who is so accurate one could, and many do, set their watch by him, passes by the First Marrien Bank. Up until this moment, the clock perched on the bank's facade has confidently announced that the current temperature is 73 degrees Fahrenheit. It then shamefully leaves thirty seconds of dead space before returning to the temperature.

As soon as Ciril passes, the clock sighs with relief and lets the whole town know that the day has started. Instantly, school buses pick children from their assigned corners. Grandfathers serving as crossing guards safely usher stragglers across the street. Bank tellers, mail carriers, paperboys, teachers, and the milkman all start their day, while Ciril walks on at the same pace, reaching his office at exactly 07:59, in time to open his business for business.

Precisely at 16:31, Ciril leaves his office, crosses the street, and enters Mo's restaurant. He smiles and nods at Marcie, the waitress, and sits at his table in the back. He orders his usual dinner of meatloaf, mashed potatoes, and green beans, washes this down with a Pepsi, never Coke, and follows it with a slice of homemade apple pie. He pays the exact cost of his meal, including a twenty-five percent tip, and leaves.

At 17:48 he enters Town Hall, turns on the lights in the conference room, and distributes the minutes from yesterday's meeting. He ensures that the pitchers and glasses are clean and filled with fresh water. Then he sits in his usual seat, reviews his notes, and compares them with the minutes from the day before.

The town council meets from 18:00 till 22:00 five days a week. At exactly 22:32, after leaving the minutes on the mayor's secretary's desk, turning off all the lights, and ensuring nobody is left in the building, Ciril locks up. He passes the bank on his way home, allowing the bank clock to double check its accuracy and shut down for the night. As does the rest of the town.

Although the weatherman comments on a very localized storm that is building over the town and suggests that people carry an umbrella, just in case, the meteorologist cannot explain the cause of the impending weather change.

Unbeknownst to Ciril, time is forming a wrinkle. That night the council meeting ends a tad early. Following his routine, he secures Town Hall at 21:17. A full hour and fifteen minutes ahead of time. As Ciril walks home and passes the bank, the clock gasps, assuming it is the one at fault. Hoping nobody notices its lapse, it resets itself before retiring for the night. Briefly, it ponders if something else is the cause, but not having fingers, it can't put one on the problem.

The town is now seriously out of step and hurries to catch up. Both traffic lights switch to their nighttime amber pattern, the washers and driers in the laundromat stop mid cycle, and the movie theater halts the show in the middle of the third reel and turns off the lights. Teenagers protest but hurry home, nonetheless. Television stations skip their ten o'clock show and switch to the empty desk of the eleven o'clock news.

Ciril, unaware of the wrinkle he may or may not have created, continues toward home at his usual unhurried but steady pace, which takes him to his front door in seven minutes, six seconds.

The wind picks up. Rain pours.

"Psst." Not being used to being addressed on the street, and surely not at this time, it takes Ciril seven and a half seconds before he realizes that someone is trying to get his attention. Among the hydrangeas in Mrs. Flowers' front yard is a … person. A person of the female persuasion, barely covered by pale blue blossoms. She's lovely, though windblown.

"Ma'am?" He clears his throat as he is not used to addressing scantily clad women. "Are you speaking to me?" He averts his eyes—mostly—from the shapely figure and offers her his umbrella. With the speed of light, a hand clasps around his wrist and hauls him into the hydrangeas.

"Now, listen. And listen closely." The enticing young lady is growing before his eyes. The cast of her eyes is ageless. She could have been molded from or been the model for Greek and Roman statues. Her voice reaches into infinity.

"Look at what you've done!"

Slowly, Ciril looks away from the imposing figure.

Though the storm is raging all around, a window onto the vastness of eternity shows chaos. Up is sideways; hot is green. Otherworldly creatures are curling over water. Dinosaurs play keep-away with Pluto. Trolls game on an I-pad. Rockettes balance on a moonbeam. Fraternity pledges rush to catch a shooting star. A big white rabbit and a Chesire grin play darts with lightning bolts. But Ciril's eyes can't look away from the unicorns that skip rope with their rainbows. He hears leprechauns curse up a storm and curse themselves when they must brave the gale to retrieve their gold coins.

"You see now?"

"No," Ciril confesses. "This doesn't add up." He rubs the back of his neck. "I don't see how I'm to blame."

"What time is it?" the woman demands.

"Time? Well, I was three point four minutes away from my home, so it must be 22:36 point six." He doesn't wear a watch, doesn't need one. He's always exactly on time.

"Try 21:21." The huff ruffles Ciril's hair.

"Preposterous!" He steps away, needing to wash his hands of the problem. "I was walking home when you rudely waylaid me into Mrs. Flowers' yard. That was at 22:36 point four or five," he gives the lady the difference in the decimal. "Don't you dare question me!" Ciril shouts over the raging storm, trying anger and posturing to overcome the unfamiliar glimmer of self-doubt.

"Oh, no!" The Athena or Juno laughs, but without mirth. "You made the mess. You fix it."

Feeling the bands, the inherent limits of time, tightening around him, he frowns up at the Amazon, who seems to still be growing. "Who are you?"

"I am Time." The storm calms to a steady downpour. "I will no longer tolerate being upstaged by you. You will respect me, will no longer ignore me or think you can best and control me. Do you understand?"

Ciril, though cringing and gasping for breath at the stricture, has to be honest. He does not know how else to respond. "No, I don't understand. I have my routines. I know the limits of time and have allocated specific amounts of the commodity to each of my activities. How am I in the wrong?"

"You, self-righteous asshat"—the sneer thunders through eternity and Ciril's head—"do not wear a watch. You, robot, do not consult time pieces, but allow time pieces to consult you. You, maggot, have presumed to be me! Just for that infraction I should, and will in time, punish you." Her smile and chuckle hold no warmth, no joy, merely a promise.

"Until then, you will vary your routines, take on extra work or leave early. You will linger over dinner, take in a movie and"—the voice becomes sultry as the hydrangea-clad, voluptuous young woman returns—"and," she sighs, "you will become my lover, savoring every second of me. Who, I ask, will be a better distraction from your rigidly timed routine than me?"

Ciril, a man, a mere mortal, does not see the calculation, the age-old seduction in her eyes when he sighs with acceptance.

It takes the town five minutes at most to realize that Ciril is no longer controlling Time. DMV employees call the next customer to their window when they damn well want to. Teachers return grades on their schedule. The milk may or may not be fresh when it is placed on the doorstep. The mail will be delivered today or another day. School bus drivers change their route without notice and leave little Skip standing on the corner, cowlick at attention.

But Ciril is unaware. His one true love, the logical and inevitable progression of Time, is no longer his to manage. Time is now his ever mercurial, demanding Mistress, the one to deliciously control him. For their first anniversary, Time gives Ciril a watch. One that ticks to its own beat.

Source: Reedsy, September 06, 2024

The Last Dragon Slayer

Late that afternoon, as he sat by the campfire, cleaning and honing his sword, Gundar heard keening coming from the mountain. He suppressed a shudder. He told himself it was the wind howling around the Tower, the monolith that dominated the otherwise empty landscape.

He hadn't set out to become a dragon slayer, or to kill any living creature. Should anyone ask him, the task sickened him. But no one asked. If he hadn't needed to settle his father's debts, he'd have walked away long ago and never looked back. Though the pay was too good, the attention and admiring glances left him cold. Too often he slipped out of town as soon as he could. Only to meet another dragon.

It seemed that each one, like the one he'd killed today and had to leave behind on the mountain, was smaller than the one before. Not that he minded the reduced resistance, but he wondered, was he killing the children? The offspring the species counted on?

He looked up when he heard the sound again. Was it the wind toying with the narrow gaps, or was it something else?

The sun was low and it wouldn't be long before night fell; the moon had already risen in the clear evening sky. Sheathing his polished sword, he walked toward the Tower. The path narrowed as it wound up the mountain. With daylight fading rapidly, and the moon his only light, he climbed and paused frequently to home in on the eerie sound.

Once again, he came to the switchback that overlooked the camp and campfire below. The hair on the nape of his neck stood up when he heard a pebble rolling off the side of the mountain. He paused. Someone, or something, was following him. Leaning close to the mountain to reduce his shadow, he heard a sob coming from within the monolith.

Making a quick decision, he turned his back to the misery within the mountain and stayed within the shadows.

"Gundar?" Melchior whispered. The young man, enamored with the fame associated with Gundar's job, had attached himself to the camp.

With a sigh, Gundar stepped forward and let the moonlight play over his features.

"Why are you following me?" he asked without censoring his anger and impatience.

"I want to help," the kid answered. "I'm your apprentice. I want to learn."

Gundar shook his head. "I never accepted you as an apprentice. I don't need your help." He didn't understand the boy's fascination with him. He was tired of killing creatures that were only defending themselves and their territory.

"I know, I volunteered," the young man acknowledged cheerfully.

"Go back, Mel. There won't be any killing tonight. Go back and sleep. I won't be long."

"Don't you hear that, Gundar? There is another one. Let me help. Give me a chance to prove myself."

"I said go back. That's an order." Gundar raised his voice.

"If I'm not your apprentice, you cannot order me," he stubbornly insisted.

"Stick around and watch me do a killing," Gundar growled.

"You will? You will let me watch?"

"Of course. It'll be your death. Wouldn't be sporting if I didn't let you watch."

"Aw, Gundar. How will I learn?"

"Better you don't. Now, go," Gundar said, shooing the youth back down the mountain.

Shoulders slumped in defeat, young Melchior turned while looking over his shoulder, still silently pleading with Gundar, who had already forgotten about the boy.

He turned his back on the valley and followed the path up. From a crevasse no wider than the depth of his chest, he saw a faint greenish light. Trying to move stealthily, he squeezed through the narrow opening. The space widened into a cave.

There, lit by soft blue glowing mosses and faint yellow glow worms, was a dragon. It was cradling the body of a smaller one on its lap. He must have made a sound, for the dragon looked up. He saw the pain and sadness in its eyes.

From the corner of his eyes, Gundar caught movement. In a flash, his sword was in his hand. When he turned to deter whoever had entered behind him, he realized that Melchior's clumsy attempt at getting an arrow from its quiver while defending against Gundar's sword had caused the arrow to penetrate his chest.

Frozen in place, Gundar watched the life seep from the young man. Guilt consumed him. He had not meant it when he'd threatened Melchior with death. He'd merely wanted to discourage the kid from following him, from idolizing him.

He sensed movement in the cave and turned to see the she-dragon walk toward him. She was obviously with child; her belly and pendulous breasts were ripe. A young dragon, no more than two and a half feet tall, hung on the mother's tail.

She pointed to the cave opening and motioned for Gundar to leave. Slowly, he walked down the mountain and slipped unseen into his tent.

The next morning, the camp is in an uproar when young Melchior is missing. Gundar leads the search party up the mountain.

Halfway between the camp and where the cave is, they find both Melchior, his chest torn open by sharp claws, and the dragon Gundar killed the afternoon before, an arrow embedded in his chest.

As the hunting party leaves to take Melchior's body home to a hero's funeral, Gundar looks back toward the mountain. He can't be sure, the way the sun lights up the façade, but he believes the she-dragon stands on the path and watches them leave.

Before the caravan reaches town, Gundar veers off the track. Nobody has seen him since.

Source: Beta Reader

Tradition

Long ago, we ran up the hill as many times a day as we could, laughing and shouting before cannonballing over the edge. But life got in the way. Whenever we passed the turn-off, we'd smile, hum our favorite tune, and suggest we go for ice cream.

Today, the walk to Lookout Point took longer, the hill seemed steeper. Hand in hand we stood at the edge, blinked at the bright blue sky, and stared at the trees beyond before looking down.

We clasped our liver-spotted hands together, smiled, nodded, and shouted when our oldest grandson took his first jump.

Source: BMS Discord. Published on 101words.org

Tropical Storm Wendy

Vern and Gladys enjoy planning. They start deliberating where to go for their annual summer vacation as soon as the Christmas decorations are packed up. They agonize over hotel versus B&B. Study the map for the best and safest route. Calculate mileage using the posted speed limits. Learn which rest stop has a gas station and clean facilities. Research and reject sights, attractions, and possible side trips. Weeks are devoted to this part of their vacation, and the planning is as much fun as the trip itself. More, maybe.

Months ahead of the trip, as soon as the booking is confirmed, they will make lists. Items will be added to the list and the decision reconsidered, only to be reversed. Weather patterns for their destination during the designated time and the probability of bad weather, or a storm, will be determined with a precision that rivals NASA's launch and reentry windows.

One week before the trip, the suitcases will be brought from the storage closet and aired out. The lists will be consulted, and packing will be initiated. Each item placed in either case will be scratched off. And at least one just-in-case case will be packed.

When they start to plan this year's vacation, Vern hems and Gladys haws. They have dutifully visited all the sights in their state—except the barrier islands. When asked, Mary Jo in Purchasing raves over the pristine beaches. Gerald in Research speaks lovingly about the many great restaurants and the fresh seafood. Felix in Accounting is very complimentary about the golf courses, and both Fred and Frederika in Marketing bring in pictures of the exotic flora and fauna.

With fingers crossed, they reserve a cabin on one of the hundreds of islands. All the official and hearsay resources they consult describe the island as warm and subtropical. Gladys hopes it won't be too warm, and Vern wonders if it will be too tropical. Silently, they pray that they won't see unfamiliar and possibly poisonous creatures slithering, buzzing, crawling, or creeping about. Or too many loud and intrusive tourists nearby. Now and then, one or the other will come close to asking if they should cancel. But then they put on a brave face and say they are looking forward to seeing the ocean.

Having read somewhere that most non-professional drivers travel on weekends, they set off early on Monday morning. As usual, they schedule four hours of travel before their first fifteen-minute comfort and refuel stop. At that time, they will each enjoy one of the sandwiches they made the night before. Then they will drive another three hours, allowing for rush-hour traffic, before checking into the cabin.

As soon as the city traffic is behind them, Gladys pushes the audio tape of *Angela's Ashes* into the deck. Raptly, they listen to the author read his work, marveling at his intonation, pacing, and sensitivity.

Only two hours into the trip, Gladys apologizes profusely and requests that Vern pull into the next rest stop. He stays with the car while she uses the facilities. When she returns to the parking lot, Vern is talking to a young lady. Worried, knowing that something must be wrong, for Vern never speaks to unfamiliar young ladies, Gladys hurries to the car.

"Hiya," the young lady, who, on closer inspection, looks younger and less ladylike, greets Gladys. "You must be Gladys. Stoked to meet you. I'm Wendy. As I was saying to Vern here, I know it's a lot to ask, but I was hoping you guys would give me a ride. My old man, well, he isn't my old man anymore, now is he? He took off without me. Left me stranded here. And I'm desperate for a ride."

Wendy takes a quick breath and continues,

"Been hanging around here for more than a day. Don't want to go off with just anyone, you know? But you two look like such a nice, comfortable, honest couple. I'd feel ever so safe riding with y'all."

Vern looks at Gladys; the lost little-boy look in his eyes is heartbreaking. Gladys stares at the girl and then at Vern. She wonders, could it be true? Are they, Vern and Gladys, a nice, comfortable, and honest couple? Yes, of course, they are. Gladys straightens her spine and lowers her shoulders. Not having a list to follow, Vern follows his wife's example.

"Where are you going, Miss …?"

"Ah, just call me Wendy, love. I have friends all over this state. You can drop me off anywhere."

Gladys takes another good look at Wendy. "We were about to have lunch …"

"Great! I know a cool place not too far from here. The owner is a great guy. I'll show you. It's not far, honestly."

"The place" is, however, not on the route Vern and Gladys had painstakingly mapped out. Wendy takes them thirty-three-and-five-eighth miles in another direction. The "cool place" is a barbecue drum next to a small, two-wheel trailer. Three picnic tables are clustered under a tree, at the side of the road.

Attending the barbecue is a bear of a man, dressed in a sleeveless sweatshirt, baggy shorts, and an apron. His big grin is permanently etched on his face. His hug is just this side of painful. Vern receives a crushing handshake and a slap on his back that starts a coughing attack. The pulled-pork sandwiches are surprisingly delicious, though very messy. The half roll of brown paper towels, possibly liberated from a gas station washroom, is barely enough to sop up all the juicy bits and pieces.

"Boss here asked if we could take lunch to his Pappy. It's not far. He'd be much obliged, and lunch will be on the house."

Both Vern and Gladys glance toward the roof of the small trailer. "On the house?" Vern asks.

"Free." She laughs. "You're funny, Vern."

Surprised at her compliment, Vern preens.

"And where does his Pappy live?" Gladys asks.

"Oh, I'll show you. Pappy is a cool guy, like you two."

Vern looks at Gladys. Gladys imagines being "cool like Pappy" and nods.

Pappy lives a bit further from the route Vern and Gladys have marked on the state map. The old man, easily ninety, is "over the moon" to get his lunch and proudly shows Vern his collection of hubcaps. And since they are "going that way", could they give Pappy and his laundry a ride to his daughter's? And the daughter would be "ever so grateful" if they could give them a ride to the nail salon where Pappy's granddaughter works. The granddaughter is "beyond desperate" for someone to drop off this one teensy package at Aunt Edna's. Aunt Edna would be "humbled and honored" if they'd give her a ride to her husband's barbecue stand. By the end of the day, Gladys and Vern have met the whole family and are back at Boss's barbecue, eating ribs. Very messy, yet very delicious, ribs.

"Aren't they just the nicest family? So close," Wendy gushes as she gnaws at the last slivers of meat. "Now, all I need is a place to crash and I'll be as done as this pig here." She wipes her mouth with a few sheets of paper towels and reaches for another rib. " But no, y'all want to be on your way. I can't ask you to …" she says as she tears at the rib.

Vern doesn't look at Gladys but focuses on his dinner.

"Ask us what?" Gladys asks carefully.

"To take me into Charleston. My friend works at a club. She'll put me up for a few nights."

"Charleston? You mean drive into Charleston?" Vern has lost his appetite because he isn't comfortable driving in big cities, especially at night.

"Don't worry, it's easy. I'll show you the back roads. No traffic whatsoever."

The club has no resemblance to the local country club Vern was once invited to, or the Knights of Columbus club their neighbors told them about, or the gentleman clubs they've seen in Sherlock Holmes movies.

Here, the music is loud. The lights are low, except the ones pointing to the empty stage with the gleaming pole where … Gladys yanks on Vern's arm. "Don't look!" she hisses.

"But …"

Wendy leads the way. "Come have a seat here at the bar. This is Jake, he's a friend of mine. Jake, these nice people have been helping me out all day. Be good to them, will you, while I look for Mercedes."

"Sure thing. What'll you have, nice people?" he asks with a smile.

Both Vern and Gladys ask for iced tea. A few minutes later, he places tall glasses in front of them. "Enjoy, nice people."

Confused, they examine the drinks while they thank Jake. Gladys looks at Vern, and Vern shrugs. These drinks look nothing like iced tea; maybe they are Cokes. Vern takes a cautious sip and declares that it doesn't taste like Coke. Gladys takes a sip and agrees. Much better, they decide. Could this be Pepsi, or maybe Dr. Pepper? When Jake puts another round in front of them, they forget to ask.

With a groan, wondering why her mouth feels as if she chewed on dead cotton balls, Gladys carefully opens her eyes and looks around the room. The thin calico curtains are drawn but are not meant to block the early morning sun. Gingerly, she crawls out of bed and leaves the room.

"Oh, good morning, love." Wendy is too loud and cheerful

by half. How has Gladys not noticed before that this child is perpetually cheerful?

"Where are we?" Gladys croaks.

"We're at the cabin you booked. Remember? Here, have a glass of juice."

Gladys nods slowly. "I remember booking it. But I don't remember checking in."

"Oh, I did that for you. I found the cooler in the trunk of the car. You brought everything to make loaded westerns. Did you enjoy yourself last night? All y'all were a big hit at the club. Really let your hair down and boogied. So cool!"

Gladys automatically touches her hair; no, it is still snug in the bun on the top of her head. She's not quite sure what "boogie" means, but Wendy says it is cool.

Gladys' eyes widen when Wendy cracks a week's worth of eggs in a bowl. "What did you say you are making?" Gladys hesitates to ask but needs must.

"Omelets. Looking at all you packed in this cooler, I'd say you're a gourmet cook, aren't you, Glad?"

After breakfast, Wendy says they must see the beach before the rain starts. The three trudge through the loose sand until they come to the water's edge. Wendy rushes ahead, prattling on about nature and feeling in tune.

Vern looks at Gladys. Gladys nods. They turn around and reach the car just as the sky opens up. They are on the road, back the way they came, straight home. One day of Wendy is as much vacation as they can take.

Next year, they might splurge and enclose their patio.

That would almost be like being on a tropical vacation year-round, wouldn't it?

Source: Beta Reader

Turkey At Large

There was a turkey who was unhappy at home.

He hid in the farmer's car, hoping to roam.

He was aghast at what he saw.

Everything flew by; he was in awe.

Wasn't he the one who flew?

The one who, when the spirit moved him, moved.

He squawked and gobbled.

He squeaked and gabbled.

But the world kept passing him.

When the farmer stopped at home,

Turkey jumped from the car.

He flapped his pathetic wings,

And called all his kin.

Don't, he said. Don't go with him.

Let him feed us, but never trust him beyond the kibble.

Source: Trudy responded to a picture Cindy Strube put on the Pets Discord channel of one of her turkeys sitting in the driver's seat of a tractor. The following is a Discord conversation between Trudy and Cindy Strube

T: Every time I try to upload the little ditty, something else uploads.

Do you want a copy of the thing? I did find the missing word.

C: Yes, please!

T: I'll try one more time. Otherwise I'll type it out.

C: On my end it just goes to … loading…

T: Ok.

C: Oh, there! It just appeared.

Ha! That's cute. They would do that…

T: Sorry had to delete a 500 word thing that keeps popping up.

Is it up on Pets (Discord channel)?

C: Yes, it finally opened.

T: oh good!

Only took 30 minutes, so not perfect. But I had fun

C: That comes through. You got the turkey "feelings".

And the turkey is driving the tractor again tonight.

Very Good Neighbors

"Oof," he grunted.

"Oh!" she squealed and blinked through the curtain of rain into a pair of pewter-grey eyes.

"You okay?" the man asked.

"Uh-huh," she said before realizing that the handsome stranger was holding her as if she were a bride he was carrying across a threshold.

She squirmed in his arms. "You can set me down now. I'm too heavy," she protested.

"Nah," he drawled. "You're just a little waterlogged." He started to lower her to the ground. When he saw that she was barefoot, he turned toward the front porch. A wry smile tugged at his mouth.

"Wait! The backdoor is open," she said while wrapping her arms tighter around his neck.

"Of course." He turned around and crossed the soggy lawn toward the back steps.

"What were you doing up there?" he asked, tipping his head toward the roof.

"The gutter is clogged," she said, as if that would be obvious.

"And the best time to clean them is in the middle of the night during a downpour." His lips twisted, trying to suppress a smile.

"Well," she bristled, "it's when I noticed."

He bit the corner of his mouth. When he set her on the back step, he let his hands rest on her hips and his eyes trail over her curves.

"Right, better go," he mumbled, pulling away. "Go take a shower," he growled as he turned around.

"Thank you," Janie whispered, distracted by the feast of his retreating figure.

He was about to slip through the opening in the hedge when she shouted.

"Hey! What's your name?"

"Quentin," he answered before disappearing inside the house next door.

"Grumpy," Janie mumbled to herself. "Good looking, but grumpy. Who needs that?"

Her phone chimed the moment she closed the kitchen door.

"He's a nice boy, Janie," her 83-year-old neighbor, Mrs. Garner, said without preamble. "Give him a chance."

"Mrs. Garner! How did you …"

"You'd still be up there, dear, if I hadn't called young Quentin," the older woman argued. "Sleep well, hon," she added and hung up.

"Thank you, Mrs. Garner," Janie said to herself.

Oh, No! Now what? Janie could feel the start of panic when she saw a construction company truck in front of her house the next day. She rushed up the lawn to where a ladder was perched against the eave. Good-natured banter and shouts came from the roof.

What was going on? Stepping out of her heels, she climbed the ladder until she could see over the edge.

Three men were scooping leaves, sticks, and old bird nests from the gutters.

"What's wrong? What are you doing?" she asked worriedly.

The three men turned toward her.

"Yes, I get it, Que." One of them grinned.

"Get down from that ladder, Janie, before you fall again," her neighbor groused as he rose to his full height and walked across the slope of the roof toward her.

"Oh, man! You are a grouch, aren't you?" she sighed, but backed down the ladder. She stopped halfway and looked up. "But why are you up there?"

"We're cleaning your gutters," he said, and told himself he was only watching her to make sure she made it down in one piece.

"Really? That's so sweet of you. Thank you. You didn't have to, you know." She smiled at him.

"We know." He should look away, but her petite body, wrapped in a sky-blue dress that highlighted all her curves, was too mesmerizing. He could still feel how tiny and delicate she'd felt in his arms last night. Last evening, he corrected himself.

"Quentin." She smiled again, sending a jolt through his

body. "Do you have plans for tomorrow?"

"Excuse me?" The change in topic brought him back to the present.

"Do you have plans for Thanksgiving dinner? Yes, of course, you do."

"No, he doesn't," Greg, his best friend and business partner, called from a corner of the roof.

"Wonderful!" She beamed. "I'm a much better cook than a roof climber. How about three o'clock? Is that okay?"

Speechless, he nodded and watched her disappear into the house.

Better cook? One can hope, Quentin thought as he stared at the back door. As he turned back to the gutter job, he saw Mrs. Garner wave at him. He waved back. Did she wink at him? Shaking his head, he walked across the roof to finish his task.

The turkey and a casserole were in the oven. The rolls were ready to go in. The table was set. Her little house was clean. The boxes that hadn't been unpacked yet were stacked in the spare bedroom. Janie looked around with satisfaction—her first house, her first dinner, and soon her first guest.

Checking the clock, she decided she had enough time for a shower before the handsome grouch would arrive. Letting the warm water sluice over her, she fantasized about Quentin. She had had an eyeful the other evening when he had deposited her on the back steps. The way his clothes had been plastered to his sculpted body!

Oh! She clasped her hand in front of her mouth, realizing that he must have had the same view of her. Blushing and grinning at the same time, she put her face under the spray.

A loud shriek jolted her heart; fear caught her breath while she froze in place. Precious moments passed before she realized that she was hearing the smoke alarm.

"No! No, no, no," she prayed. Not here. Not now. Not her dinner. Not in her own little house. Turning off the water, wrapping herself in a towel, she rushed from the bathroom into the kitchen.

Coughing against the smoke billowing from the oven, she reached for the handle, but a hand pulled her away from the stove.

"No! Don't touch," Quentin shouted. With one arm around her waist, he used a potholder to turn off the oven. Pulling the pin on the extinguisher, he doused the fire inside the oven.

"Dinner," she sighed. "It's ruined!"

When he was satisfied that the fire was out, he turned around and wrapped her small, wet body in his arms.

"Sh, now. Hush," he soothed her, rubbing his hand down her hair and over her back. "It's okay. You're okay."

"I screwed up again," she sobbed.

"It probably was the stove's fault," he assured her.

"Why are you early?" She looked up at him. "And where did that come from?" She pointed at the empty extinguisher.

"I came a little early to see if I could help." And because

he couldn't wait to see her again. "And this was supposed to be your housewarming present." He smiled wryly.

"You did help." She rested her head against his chest. "And that was better than a bottle of wine."

On impulse, he kissed her forehead. "Get dressed. We'll order pizza at my place."

"Pizza for Thanksgiving." She shook her head. "Mom would be appalled. Not surprised, of course, but appalled." She chuckled, her natural cheerfulness bouncing back as she walked to the bathroom.

Quentin smiled while he opened the kitchen window. He was looking forward to keeping a close eye on his new neighbor for both their benefits.

Source: Jas Family

Waiting For A Tow Truck

"Well, you see, it's an STD, right?"

Jason snorted but kept listening while he ran his hands down my leg.

"The male of the species, the infectious agent, or culprit, will deposit one or more parasites in the female. Left untreated, this condition will have two stages. During the first, or acute stage, the parasite will live off the female's body and flourish."

Jason chuckled, but I ploughed on, trying not to wince when he found another one.

"The female's lower abdomen will distend to unsightly proportions. After about 36 weeks—of course, this period varies between species—the parasite will spontaneously expel itself."

I paused, holding up my finger, making Jason wait for the punchline.

"Then the disease goes over to the chronic, incurable, and ultimately fatal stage called motherhood."

I smirked.

"Holy crap!" Jason laughed. "You thought long about that one, did you?"

"Yes, but it was mostly for humanitarian reasons, you know? I wasn't very fond of myself as a kid or teen and couldn't see sending another one like me into the world. So,

I skipped that life experience. And not having kids gave me lots of time to work out that theory."

We were sitting in the grass, leaning against a tree on the side of a mountain pass. The tires had spun out on a tricky hairpin turn. Now the car was snugly resting in a clump of clingy, prickly plants.

"Why didn't you have any kids?" I asked when it was my turn to pull thorns from his back.

He scoffed. "You already had your tubes tied when we met."

I laughed. "You had plenty of time to sow oats before then."

He hissed when I dislodged a stubborn thistle. We were quiet while, like monkeys, we plucked brambles and chiggers off each other.

"Do you believe in fortunetelling and all that stuff?" I asked.

"Not really. Why?"

"Years ago, a friend dragged me along to a fortune teller slash palmist slash medium. That friend wanted me to hold her hand. Sorry," I said while pulling a stubborn thorn from his shoulder. "Her other hand," I clarified.

Jason sniggered.

"Since I was there anyway, I had my fortune told. Why not, I thought. Hold on, this one is nasty."

"What did she tell you?" Jason asked, trying to distract himself.

"She told me to beware of hairpins."

"She didn't," he scoffed and hissed through the sting.

"Yeah, I didn't get it at the time, but I do now."

We grinned at each other when we heard the rumble of a truck echo between the mountains.

Source: Beta Reader

We Were Not Amused

We grant you this interview and caution you not to interrupt while we relate the events. And please put away your quill and parchment.

Two days prior to the event, we embarked on a quest for solitude and reflection to review our position, its value, freedoms, and restrictions.

We intended to sleep rough—we believe that is the correct expression—and live off the generosity of the land. To that end, we opted to use an unmarked carriage on less-traveled roads and stay in simple taverns.

However, we did not see the harm in allowing a charming young couple to share our space for a few miles. Full of enthusiasm, they told us about a fair they planned to attend. We believe they used the term "thumbing their way" to the venue. We found this to be an inventive and economic concept.

We shared our modest meal with them and retired for the night. We do not know where the young couple spent the night.

This morning, we experimented with shaving our beard using a straight razor. We nicked ourselves a few times. When we broke our fast, the young lady offered to do the task properly. We declined, explaining that we enjoyed the learning process. But in truth, we are not accustomed to being touched by others.

As we rode on, they chatted incessantly about the various activities they planned to indulge in and the dances they hoped to perform. We merely smiled, nodded, and tried to understand that their world and interests were far different from ours.

Although we were beginning to regret having allowed them to ride with us, we did not wish them any harm. Not at that time.

Upon returning to our vehicle after our midday repast, the young lady accosted our driver and rushed to take the reins; meanwhile, the young man threatened us with our own straight razor. We prepared to defend ourselves, but he lunged at us. A tussle ensued. Blood was spilled—ours. It was patently clear that the young man was the better fighter. We assume that his education had not been limited to a sparring ring. Upon our return home, we discussed our less-than-stellar defense skills with our trainer.

As we watched the couple drive away in our vehicle, we sent for assistance.

Earlier, you referred to the young couple as our friends. We hesitate to classify them as acquaintances, but if we must, we will say that they are friends we don't see anymore. You see, officer, we shall not press charges against the youths because our guards have already taken the culprits into custody. They will enjoy the hospitality of our dungeons for many years to come.

We apologize if our misfortune has inconvenienced you and your men in any way. We, your sovereign, are most grateful for your assistance, loyalty, and continued discretion.

That will be all, sir.

Source: Beta Reader

What Lies Beneath

Summer 1972.

"Road trip!" Pam screamed over the sound of the juke box. She had shoved her chair aside, since there was no dancefloor in this hole-in-wall bar, her arms in the air, hips bumping and grinding to the beat. Feet barely moving. After half a pitcher, she could sway her hips or move her feet. She opted for swaying to Otis Redding.

"Wastin' time!" Barb was still capable of doing a fair lip-sync of *Sittin' On the Dock of the Bay*. Pam was a tad too wasted to remember all the words.

Fancying themselves the last hippies, the two girls planned to leave their homes in Georgia and head for the Frisco Bay. A few weeks earlier, Barb had bought a '58 VW van—orange, of course. Whoever had owned Old Orange before had taken out the rear benches and built a sleeping platform, leaving plenty of storage underneath.

About ten days into the trip, by the time they came to Houston, they realized that the air hose, a vital necessity to cool the engine, would not stay where it was supposed to be. So, taking the southern route through the desert was out of the question. So, they turned right toward Dallas.

Old Orange had a few other minor quirks. For instance, the radio only worked in third and fourth gear. The windshield wipers only went one way. After each swipe, whoever was in the passenger seat needed to pound on the windshield to dislodge the wiper. Orange's top speed was 50 mph if the wind was at their back, a little faster if going downhill. The starter had left them in New Orleans. Which showed remarkable good taste for a starter and made Pam the designated pusher. In Dallas, they learned the expensive lesson that transmissions require fluids.

They spent a week in a tiny village at Lake Superior shore, where the main entertainment was going to the dump and watching the bears feed. Pointing west again, the plan was to bypass Denver and go to Aspen. Orange was willing but unable to keep the minimum speed of 40 mph while climbing up I-70. Once again, a detour was needed. They headed north into Wyoming before turning west again.

Two days later, they left Jackson Hole after breakfast and entered the Grand Tetons with its raw, relatively young peaks. Mid-morning, they pulled in at a rest stop next to a small lake. It was mid-June; the north slope had been warmed by the sun for several weeks and was carpeted with wildflowers. Every color in the rainbow, and all the ones in between. The south side was still holding on to patches of snow. This contrast, on either side of the still water, reflecting the blue sky, was breathtaking.

While Barb was coaxing enough life from the Coleman stove to heat water, Pam stretched her legs. Avoiding the clumps of snow and sludge, she made her way up the south hill. Feeling a rumble in the ground, she was stunned at the sight when she looked over the top of the hill.

Animals! Moose, elk, deer, rabbits, skunks, buffalo, and the odd wolf all running eastward. Pam was a city girl but even she thought this was strange. None of the animals paid any attention to her or each other. They ran, stampeding across the meadow, as fast as their legs would move.

Worried, she returned to the van. Barb listened and shrugged. "It's nothing," she said. "If there was a fire, they would have closed the park. Let's have our coffee and go on."

Pam wasn't so sure but took her word for it.

Soon they drove on, admiring the breathtaking majesty that are the Tetons. By early afternoon, they entered the visitor's center of Yellowstone Park. Right on time, which meant too late to get front row seats, or rather front row standing spots to watch the show.

While the summer intern was giving a play-by-play, Old Faithful did its thing.

"Well, folks, thank you for coming. If you want to see it again, please come back in …" Old Faithful spewed again.

"Wow!" the kid gushed. "That's a first."

And again, another plume of sulfuric steam erupted. The intern stood staring, mouth open. Everybody felt the rumble. Some may have been more alarmed than others, but they all felt it.

Old Faithful was quiet for a few minutes. People dared to exhale in relief. Pam just wanted to grab Barb and run, but she didn't. She stayed with the other tourists and stared.

And then another spurt. No, that's not the right word. A geyser, a flume … Oh, hell! Let's just call it what it was. An eruption! The hot, sulfuric steam bubbled up and erupted, overstepping its recognized boundaries and spraying over the poor, hapless tourists who were standing on the eastern boardwalk.

This time, Pam dragged her friend away. Barb jumped in the driver's seat while Pam, since that was her job, pushed the old relic off. As soon as Barb was able to turn the engine over, Pam ran and jumped in the passenger seat. People were screaming, running, elbowing, pushing, and stumbling over each other. Some looked like extras in a horror movie, faces burned, clothing melting to their skin.

Only this was real.

She didn't want to watch, didn't want to see. But it's like a massive pile up; you just have to. Pam gasped when she saw the head.

Just think of the slobbering, angry head, the poster child of the Jurassic Park movies, the face only a mother could love. That's what reared up out of the boiling water. It had had eons to incubate and mature. And that day it was ready to claim its heritage.

If they'd taken the time, they might have wondered how many of those creatures had laid their eggs in the warm springs of Yellow Stone. How many eggs had survived the long winter that followed the meteor impact? The one that extinguished this one's mommy and daddy?

They didn't have to ask or wonder because just as Barb was able to back up without running over anyone, another one crawled out. This one had wings and within minutes took flight. Fully grown. Or, at least, hopefully it was fully grown. If this was just a baby, it could grow up to be much bigger than a jumbo jet. Much, much bigger.

The lake—that famous tourist attraction, that placid aqua blue, edged in yellow circle—was now a churning cauldron with prehistoric critters peeking out before clambering ashore. Screeching, howling, knocking over, crushing anything in their paths.

"Go, please go!" Pam begged.

"I can't!" Barb cried. "I want to, but I can't make myself drive over anyone."

"If you don't, they will." Pam pointed to the creatures that were crawling out of the water.

"Oh, shit! Oh shit, oh shit," Barb summed up the situation.

Though they knew it was time to haul ass, and even then, it might be too late, they sat there in the deceptive safety of Old Orange and stared as one grotesque beast after another crawled out of the boiling water.

"Go," Pam whimpered. "Go, please. Go, Barb!" She nudged, shook, punched. Did what she could to make Barb wake up. "Go!" she screamed.

With a curse and a shudder, Barb put her foot on the gas and jumped forward. *Don't stall, don't stall, don't stall,* Pam prayed as she turned backward in her seat and watched the first tree burst spontaneously into flames. "Faster, Barb, faster."

Barb was a good driver. That day, she turned into an excellent demolition derby driver. Aggressively, she drove around everybody, forced people into ditches and off the side of the mountain. She prayed, the act of contrition— "Oh, my Lord God. I am heartily sorry for offending Thee ."—all the way into Idaho.

They had grumbled the day before, when the gas station in Jackson Hole had gouged them. When the pump claimed to have put twelve gallons into a half-full ten-gallon tank, then charged them the usury price of forty-two cents per gallon for the privilege. But at least they had a full tank, and they were going downhill, which in the little old van was a plus, a great plus.

Maybe those flying creatures were colorblind and couldn't see orange, because cars left and right, front and back of them were picked up and dribbled like basketballs, rolled like marbles, stepped on like empty beer cans. But Barb weaved and bobbed and evaded their games.

It didn't take long, just a few millennia, to make it to Shoshone Ice Caves, where they huddled with hundreds of other refugees till the National Guard came to tell them that it was safe to leave the cave.

Pam and Barb never made it to San Francisco. Old Orange threw a rod the next day.

Source: Reedsy, May 03, 2024

Whispers

"Did you hear the latest? Oh, my! Do sit down, have a cup of tea. You have met Lady Farnsworth, have you not? Exactly! At the Wendtworth ball. Yes. Her garden is legendary. Or so I've heard. I don't really know anyone who has seen it firsthand. With the exception of Lady Creason, but all she will say about it is that the garden is simply magnificent, divine."

"No, really, it's almost too much. She does it herself! Can you imagine? I shudder to think … Oh, the horror! Dirtying her gloves as she digs in the soil, as if she's a common maid! My, my! Do you think she sinks to her knees in the dirt?"

"Oh, it's all anyone can talk about. More tea? Yes, of course, let me ring for a fresh pot."

"And Lord Cecil being so sickly, he had to retire to the country, don't you know? Can you believe that she has remained here in town, while her husband might very well be on his deathbed? At least Lord John is keeping vigil. She's not showing him the proper respect, is she? Not at all, at all."

"Oh my! The scandal! But what could one expect from such an unsuitable match?"

"Tut-tut."

***

Three years ago, Lady Martha Worthmore, age eighteen, had been presented. As all young girls will, she had looked forward to all the parties and balls, the flirtations, a stolen kiss. Not surprisingly, like all young girls, she had dreamed of a love match. After all, who'd want to be part of a mere "suitable" alliance? However, no offers had been made in the first few weeks.

"Not to worry," Lady Eagers, her chaperone, had assured her. "Many young ladies do not get a suitable offer till their second or even third Season."

However, Martha's father, Lord John Worthmore, was not of the same opinion or as patient. Thus, when Lord Cecil Farnsworth, an old bachelor friend of Lord Worthmore, made an offer, he accepted immediately on his daughter's behalf.

Despite Martha's protests, Lord John would not renege on the bargain. Even before her first Season had run its course, Lady Martha Worthmore became Lady Cecil Farnsworth. Married to a man thirty-one years her senior.

For three years, Lady Martha and Lord Cecil divided their time between the townhouse during the Season and Lord Farnsworth's sprawling, drafty estate house, somewhere off the beaten path in Durham.

Lord Farnsworth had not bothered to consummate the marriage and rarely deigned to speak to her directly. Of course, dinner invitations to reciprocate hospitality had to be extended. Thus, once every month or two during the Season Martha and Cecil would be in the same room, be it at opposite ends of the table.

Having little else to occupy her time, Lady Martha took it upon herself to bring the neglected garden attached to the town house back to life. To that end, she recently charged the butler, Mansort, with hiring a competent gardener. With increasing regularity, she declined to accompany her husband to the country. She was quite content in the smaller, but comfortable, house in town.

***

Three months ago, Lady Martha once again, sipping her morning tea, admired her garden. To be honest, the man cultivating and maintaining all this beauty was much more interesting than the garden itself. After all, the roses he was tending just beyond the breakfast room window had just barely begun to sprout.

He was—she swallowed a sigh—quite muscular. She couldn't help but feel that he simply exuded an aura of strength, confidence, and capability. Tilling, weeding, and mulching was apparently hot work, even this early in spring, for he had put his coat aside and rolled up his shirt sleeves. Oh, my! He straightened, lifted his cap, wiped his brow with the cravat he had stuffed in the waist of his trousers. She could see the damp ends of his russet-colored hair before he replaced his cap.

She was incapable of stifling another sigh when he threw his head back and drank deeply from the flask that had been tucked in one of his pockets. She shamelessly allowed her eyes to drift down to the few loosened buttons at his throat, caress the expanse of his chest, and dip further down to … Oh! Surely that wouldn't do. Quickly she snapped her eyes back to his face. Just in time to see him watching her. She told herself that she imagined the small smile and quick wink before he returned to his labors.

"Ah, yes." Lady Sarah Creason, Martha's long-time friend and confidante, groaned. "If my roses were that well-tended, I might even consider cultivating them in my boudoir."

"Surely you jest." Martha tried to sound outraged, but the idea did have its merits.

Martha's father, a frequent guest, and Lord Cecil spent many hours in the library. Martha had been told that they were playing chess. Since her husband did not concern himself with her activities, she did not think twice about their many games of chess.

That afternoon, Lord Worthmore, after he had greeted Martha, joined Lord Cecil in the library. Unconcerned with the gentlemen's game, Martha took a shawl against the chill spring breeze and strolled through the garden. There, near the gazebo, she spotted the gardener. She hesitated, feeling a tell-tale blush flush her cheeks, but she ploughed on.

"Good afternoon, Mr. Garreth."

Garreth doffed his cap. "Afternoon, milady."

"What are you planting here?" She pointed to the small patch of freshly tilled earth.

"I had thought this might be a good spot for fragrant herbs, like lavender and mint. But if you have a preference …" He smiled as he looked at her.

Martha blushed under his gaze. There was something about his voice, the musical lilt and cadence to his speech. "Pansies." She smiled shyly. "I quite fancy pansies. They remind me of velvet."

He nodded. "Very well. I'll be sure to include pansies,

milady."

She should move on and allow him to return to his work. But she was reluctant to part company.

"Milady." He seemed hesitant to speak. "There is one section of the garden I have difficulty with. Could you take a look and advise me?"

"But of course." All shyness forgotten. Someone needed her assistance; she'd be happy to give it.

"There is a bush, it's just in front of the library window. I would be obliged if you'd give it a look and ponder the situation, Milady."

"I will do so, right this minute, Mr. Garreth."

Marth strode off in the direction of the house, specifically the west side where the library was located. She could not see any dead, dying, or distressed plants in the bed, but when she looked up, she gasped.

Just on the other side of the library window were her father and husband. However they were not engrossed in a chess match.

"I see you found the problem, Milady."

"Yes, Mr. Garreth. You'd best move on, lest you're seen and risk being fired," She advised him.

Approximately three weeks had passed since Martha had inspected her yard. She had instructed Cook to prepare supper for three and invited her father to partake, thus ensuring that her husband would attend as well.

When the first course was cleared and the fish served,

Martha paused and nodded at Mansort, who left the dining room, ushering the valets ahead of him. When the room was occupied by just the three of them, Martha took another bite, chewed daintily, and swallowed.

"About three weeks ago, I learned something," she began. "I learned that my father has a birthmark in the shape of the continent of Africa on his left buttock." She nodded, letting that sink in. "And you, Milord, do not. However, I now understand why many of your shirt sleeves are ink stained."

She indulged in a sip of wine. "Gentlemen, I do not care how you wish to spend your time together, but I believe that there are many people who would be scandalized and affronted, if not downright sickened, at the thought alone. Not to mention that the activity is illegal. Hopefully that law will change at some point in the future.

She calmly took another bite. Having had several weeks to come to terms with the situation, she had charted a course. "In that light, I suggest that one or both of you urgently retreat to the country for your health before anyone learns the truth."

Since both men were still speechless, she took another bite and a sip of wine before she rang the bell for Mansort, asking him to bring the items she had handed him earlier. She then turned back to her husband and father.

"I will not join you in the country, of course. Therefore, I shall need funds at my disposal to maintain the house, the stables, yard, and social obligations. Ah, thank you, Mansort." She turned back to her dinner guests. "Mansort is placing contracts in front of you. All you have to do is sign to place the townhouse in my name along with the annual sum I have stipulated. There will be no trustees managing my affairs, of course. We will all live separate lives and your secret will be safe with me."

***

"Did you hear? Surely, you must have. Is there no end to her brazenness? With both her husband and father in the country, awaiting Lord Cecil's demise, Lady Martha has now brought plants in the house! Oh, yes! I have it on the best authority. In every room, no less. Even in her boudoir. My stars!"

"She does look well, doesn't she? I might go as far and say she's flourishing."

Source: Reedsy, June 09, 2024 (Shortlisted)

Blue Marble Storytellers

Remembering Trudy

The following is a series of quotes and other conversations people of the Blue Marble Storyteller community had with Trudy.

Trudy's opening comments in the Blue Marble Storyteller Discord.

Trudy: *Hi, This is Trudy. I finally made it. Trying to figure out how this works.*

…

Trudy: *where do I find conversations. And to be perfectly honest, theses moving "cutie" are quite distracting, but I'll get used to them, if I have to.*

[Ed: The "cutie" is the welcome animations]

…

Trudy: *Well, allow me to introduce myself. Trudy Jas, from Cincinnati, Oh. Originally from The Netherlands. Have been entering on Reedsy for almost a year. It's quite addicting.*

Russell Norman

The last text conversation I had with Trudy:

Trudy: *Thanks I will let you go. And I will go back to fantasizing I'm 27. Talk to you later.*

Michelle Oliver

Trudy was such a wonderful person. She was full of wit and sass. We were having great conversations about getting older and how that feels. This pearl from Trudy is a result of me moaning about feeling down about hot sweats and body aches.

Trudy: *Don't have to explain to me. At 73 I've been there, done that. It's like puberty in reverse. The only thing I can tell you that that part will get better. (and then the rest of the body falls apart) sorry. Positives? mammos and pap smears will stop, underarm hair growth will slow (besides who can see the grey?) Negatives? weight gain, hair loss, except on chin and upper lip (no, we will not call it beard and moustache) incontinence, painful intercourse,*

Oh, sorry, you were already depressed.

Anna Sharples

The last conversation I had with Trudy, emblematic of her curiosity and imagination:

Trudy: *Just one more question (and yes, I do live under* *a rock, have little idea what "young-uns" do these days, but am willing to learn)*

These drunk groomsmen don't really throw axes off the bus, do they?

Anna: *No, thankfully!! There are indoor axe-throwing places. I've not been but I've seen them in a few cities in the last five years. It's an activity a bit like bowling or indoor golfing except you throw axes, I think*

Trudy: *That is still a scary thought. Thanks.*

<u>Deidra Lovegren</u>

I first met Trudy by email sent on Tue, Jan 2, 2024:

Trudy:

Hi,

My name is Trudy Jas. I am one of your 3000+ followers on Reedsy. I read your feedback to Jack Kimball on his recent story.

I hope you have the time to take a look at one of my stories and tell me how I can improve.

Any feedback is appreciated.

Thank you.

Trudy Jas

Then a comment on one of my Reedsy stories:

Trudy:

Jan 26, 2024

I'm showing either my age or my general ignorance. I understand tripping, I understand balls. Together, though …

Loved the nuisance calls, especially the little boys.

Alexis Araneta

Trudy always had such sharp wit and was a master of making everyone laugh … including through innuendo.

So, here's one from a Discord discussion on an all-romance bookstore:

Russell Norman: *Hey Alexis, they created a bookstore just for you….*

Alexis: *Thing is, the fact it's called Saucy Books is kind of givng me pause. I'm kind of more into Sense and Sensbility, not Sex and Sensuality.*

Trudy: *That's okay, Alexis. I'll pick up the slack.*

Alexis: *shocked cat GIF*

Trudy: *Down, Kitty, down. LOL.*

Most of my chats with Trudy were quite long and covered a range of topics so pulling out bits that might be suitable is difficult but this is part of the last conversation I had with her, on her birthday, and it really made me smile. . .

Trudy on drinking:

Kay: *are you doing anything today?*

Trudy: *my neighbors invited me over for pizza. Yum*

Kay: *that sounds great*

Trudy: *gotta love the gooey grease, washed down with cheap wine. oh, wait that was college. It'll be good wine this time. LOL*

Kay: *my grandad once found my grandmother passed out on her keyboard after she drank half a bottle of southern comfort not realising how strong it was*

Trudy: *nothing wrong with a glass or two/three*

Kay: *he thought it was hilarious that she had key imprints in her forehead*

Trudy: *that's like drinking moonshine with sugar LOL there used to be - maybe still is - Mad Dog 20/20. 20 proof for wine = Wine. a small bottle will do it.*

Kay: *oh my god - I used to drink that stuff when I was a teenager. horrible synthetic fruit flavours. like kiwi and orange and lime*

Trudy: *LOL so you trained your liver early*

Kay: *every friday night LOL we also used to drink*

Thunderbird – did you ever have that?

Trudy: *Yup. I would steal dad's brandy. Purely for medicinal reason, as a sleep aid.*

Kay: *of course hahahaha I'm mostly a cider drinker now*

Trudy: *Mom had this waterford bottle/vase. would hold no more than a thimble or two. I'd fill it when I was alone at home and sip it. Still have the little thing. Nah, the good stuff for me. Scotch, or a wine that cost more than $10*

Kay: *I cant drink spirits really – they make me feel a bit sick. maybe because of one too many tequila parties at university. I do like the odd cocktail if its mixed with something sweet – like a long island iced tea or a cherry bakewell*

Trudy: *that would do it. Got sick on bourbon (southern comfort or something like it) can't stand the smell of it anymore.*

Kay: *my brother is a Jack Daniels drinker – I cant stand the stuff*

Trudy: *Funny. one family dinner I was sitting next to my brother who was drinking Jack D and I was drinking Johnny W. The waitress got us confused. I smelled the difference immediately. One doesn't really want to be that much of an expert. Stick with cider.*

I found this so funny (side note—Havilah is my baby):

Trudy: *Once I have the picture in my head, the story is finished except for the witing. If I can't see the middle and end it may never be born. have a lot of those floating my mind*

Trudy: *ready for 1030 words of soft porn - unedited?*

Nicole: *I may have to read behind my fingers lol.*

Trudy: *well, just don't let your oldest read it - of course hubby is welcome to enjoy.*

Nicole: *Sorry, I've got a youth group I'm prepping for. So I skimmed over. I think it looks great. You wrote the young man's perspective well. Not overdone (like so many others). It has a mystical feel, like maybe it could be a dream or shes's a witch. The vibes are great.*

Trudy: *Yeah! I hope you turned Havilah around, so she didn;t get the wrong vibes. LOL. Go and have fun with the kids. You are Mother Earth!*

Trudy: *And btw. I'll go with the dream or witch bit, but rather like the cougar idea too. An old woman can hope, you know.*

Keba Ghardt

Trudy: *thanks!!!! I'm always – no – I never know what I'm doing. I think I have a great story and get "meh" and then I think, this is crap, but it's what I have, and people go yay!*

So I don't know anymore.

I don't do dragons and zombies. I don't do cyborgs and witches. I don't do what I can't see or feel myself. So, some places are off limits. But I keep writing.

Laurie Spellman

Trudy on writing romance

Trudy: *How are you doing with your date story? Sorry, it's too early, isn't it? And you have a big day girl. Let me know when you're ready. Here's mine.*

Laurie: *I went through it and gave suggestions. I think you need to build up the app more in the story. They jump too quickly into banter after she realizes she's been catfished. This is still a romance and should follow the beats of a romance arc. I'm attaching the beat sheet by Gwendolyn Hayes as a reference. I hope this helps.*

Trudy: *Thanks, Laurie. Appreciate it. BTW what does catfished mean?*

Laurie: *Being catfished means being deceived by someone who creates a false online identity to trick you. This can involve using fake photos and information to impersonate someone else, with the intent of defrauding* *or manipulating the victim.*

Trudy: *Thanks. So, not very romantic.*

Laurie: *Right so she needs to be mad then soften.*

Trudy: *Yeah, it's a mess. it's been 50 years, at least since I've been on a date. Totally out of practice. LOL*

I revisited the wonderful Trudy on Reedsy and found these gems.

Comments:

Trudy Jas left a comment on your book Thirteen Dots:

Don't feel bad. I didn't understand the Matrix either. But the anxiety, fear, depair came through loud and clear.

Jan 06, 2025

Trudy Jas left a comment on your book Noble Prickly Love:

Fabulous Fir Fondness, Passionate Pine Ponderings, Eternal Evergreen Emotions. Lovely Love story, Laurie.

Dec 17, 2024

Trudy Jas left a comment on your book Ton Talk:

Never having heard of Julia Quinn or Bridgerton, I was thoroughly lost in your gossip column. Assuming that your veiled references alluded to characters in the books/ show. Having said that, it sounded authentic, barbs and all.

Laurie, gossip is actually a stretch for me. I always forget what people tell me.

Jun 09, 2024

Recipes

Trudy was a sharing and caring person. The following was a recipe she provided for Poffertjes.

Poffertjes are a traditional Dutch batter cake:

3dl milk, 20 g yeast, 400 g flour (or if you know how to adjust for self rising, have at it), 2 eggs, salt, 200 g raisins, 50g candied fruit, 1/2 apple, oil, confectioners sugar.

Disolve yeast in a little luke warm milk till a smooth paste (or follow directions on package, my cook book is from 1974). Mix flower, yeast, eggs, milk, and salt until dough is smooth. Cover, set aside in warm place, and let rise for an hour.

Rinse and dry raisins, chop candied fruit and apple. Add to dough and mix (mom broke several wooden spoons doing this. It gets quite thick and heavy)

Using 2 wet spoons, drop dollops of dough in hot oil, then fry till brown and fully cooked on the inside. Dust with powdered sugar.

Happy New Year.

Acknowledgements

The publishers wish to acknowledge the wonderful support received from the Blue Marble Storytellers community in compiling this collection of stories.

A special mention goes to Cindy Strube, Kay Northbridge, and Ruth M Smith for their tireless efforts to track down all the stories known to have been written by Trudy over the past couple of years.

Once again on another Blue Marble project, a heartfelt thank-you to Anna Sharples for her great editing, proof-reading, and consummate all-round sharp-eyed grammar skills.

Finally, a big thank-you to the Jas family, and specifically Trudy's brother Hein and niece Anouk, for their support of this project.

www.ingramcontent.com/pod-product-compliance
Lightning Source LLC
Chambersburg PA
CBHW072109300726

48975CB00003B/762